A
Harlequin
Romance

OTHER
Harlequin Romances
by ROUMELIA LANE

Many of these titles are available at your local bookseller, or through the Harlequin Reader Service.

For a free catalogue listing all available Harlequin Romances, send your name and address to:

HARLEQUIN READER SERVICE,
M.P.O. Box 707, Niagara Falls, N.Y. 14302
Canadian address: Stratford, Ontario, Canada N5A 6W4

or use order coupon at back of books.

THE TENANT OF
SAN MATEO

by

ROUMELIA LANE

Harlequin Books

TORONTO • LONDON • NEW YORK • AMSTERDAM • SYDNEY • WINNIPEG

Original hardcover edition published in 1976
by Mills & Boon Limited

ISBN 0-373-01984-X

Harlequin edition published June, 1976

Printed In U.S.A.

CHAPTER ONE

A FRESH breeze blew across the decks of the *San Carlo*
as she ploughed towards the leaden horizon. The
swirling green troughs ahead rose up with flaring talons
in her passing, all eager to claim her into their fathom-
less depths. But the *San Carlo* was a modern stream-
lined vessel who took domination of the sea as her
right. Her bulwarks and timbers creaking with disdain, she rode the waves like a queenly dowager with a
string of tiresome pekinese at her heels.

Faye gazed out from the shelter of glass partitions
on the deck, feeling pleased with herself. She had
never expected to obtain an afternoon sailing and the
elegant Italian line was a pleasant surprise after the
clumsy, ponderous Spanish ferries with their untili-
tarian comforts in which she had been accustomed to
making the overnight crossing.

It was true after her drive down from England
through France and Spain she could have done with a
few hours' rest. But she was far too impatient to hang
about cooling her heels on the docks in Barcelona,
when Majorca beckoned a mere hundred and fifty
miles away to the south. When she had been told that
the *San Carlo*, recently in from Genoa, was about to
make the trip to the island she had torn off to buy a
ticket and later driven her dusty old Morris aboard
with a jubilant flourish.

Now she stood and watched the mountains of spray
breaking over the bows of the ship feeling the same
old thrills that she always felt at this stage of her
journey; although the thought that this time there
would be no one waiting for her on her arrival was a
slightly sobering one. And there was no denying that

as the sky darkened with approaching night and the cold breezes found their way through her thick coat, she experienced the same qualms and uncertainties that all wanderers feel when striking out for the first time on their own. However, these were quickly dispersed by the bouncing optimism which had inspired her to pack up and leave the cosy life she had always known a thousand miles behind her. She laughed at herself now and faced the wind roaring over the decks with renewed vigour. She was on her way to Majorca. What could possibly go wrong on such a paradise island!

It was the first spattering of heavy raindrops which sent her scurrying for shelter. Along with the other strolling passengers caught in the shower she tumbled amidst gusts of laughter into the lighted indoors.

Swept along in the animated atmosphere, her own happy excitement refusing to let her relax, Faye explored, with countless others, the mysterious doorways, passageways and staircases leading off from the main passenger deck. She browsed around the duty-free shop, sighing at the beautiful but madly expensive gifts which were way out of her reach, and peered through glass portholes at the restaurant doing a modest trade.

She soon learned to avoid the masculine element aboard, knowing all too well that no one is more forthright in his advances than the Spanish male. In narrow spaces and wood-panelled confines, laughing-eyed Romeos would block her path with expressions of startled delight, but Faye moved on ignoring, with a twinkle, the stir caused by her wide-set hazel eyes and mane of red hair.

The lounges were fuller than ever when she arrived, with people who had booked cabins for the journey and were now coming up for an evening drink. Faye wandered around despairingly. She would have given anything to sit down, but every armchair, wall-sofa and padded seat seemed to be occupied. She turned abruptly from where she had been searching with her gaze near the bar and almost fell over someone's feet.

'Oh, *perdón!*' she exclaimed, feeling a toe crunch under her shoe.

'That's all right,' the man on the bar stool grinned wincingly, 'I've got another foot.'

'Oh, you're English! I'm terribly sorry....'

The attractive woman on the next stool nudged the man and said drily, 'The girl's looking for a seat, Bart. Now's your chance to demonstrate the chivalry of the British.'

'Oh, really.... No!' Faye protested as the man rose goodnaturedly. His wife took Faye's wrist and pulled her on to the stool, adding with a conspiratorial smile, 'Take it. He's been loafing on his bunk in the cabin all afternoon. It will do him good to stretch his legs for a while.'

Taking the ribbing all in good part, the man man-oeuvred himself among the crush at the bar and re-lieved Faye of her coat. His wife said smilingly, 'You're like us, I expect.' She viewed the noisy scene around them with a sardonic light. 'You're convinced there won't be a soul travelling on a January afternoon. You get to the boat and what do you find? The thing's packed!' She tilted an eyebrow. 'Where do they all come from and where do they all go, that's what I want to know.'

'Everybody else is probably asking the same question and including us,' her husband grinned.

'Well, we have to get home, don't we?' his wife ex-claimed with goodnatured amusement.

'Precisely,' came the smiling reply.

'You're not going to tell me that all these people live in Majorca!'

The shoulders beside her hunched patiently. 'We've got to remember it's a holiday island, and if it wasn't

7

we wouldn't have a home to go to. Now what would the young lady like to drink?'

As the humorous brown gaze came to rest on her Faye said shyly, 'Well ... er ... I was just going to have a coffee.'

The woman eyed her with a merry gleam. 'You *can't* just sit and sip coffee on an uproarious occasion like this,' she teased above the tremendous din around them. 'How about a vodka and lime, and while we're waiting to be served we'll introduce ourselves.'

'All right,' Faye laughed, her shyness quickly evaporating in the friendly atmosphere.

Bart and Greta Templeton ran a small hotel in Majorca. They had been to Barcelona for a few days' shopping and were returning to prepare for the spring holiday season which would soon be upon them. Faye learned all this as they sat chatting cosily over their drinks. She had liked the couple on sight. She might even have described them as a homely pair if they hadn't been so attractive to look at. They possessed a maturity, which couldn't by any stretch of the imagination have been called middle-age.

Greta wore her ash-blonde hair expertly cut in the modern style, and was exquisitely made up. She was wearing an obviously expensive dress in a pale blue material and a matching long-sleeved jacket, and a chunky silver bracelet on her wrist.

Her husband was no less striking in his own way. He wore a look of perpetual contentment, and they were obviously a pair who had made the right choice marriage-wise and wanted nothing more from life.

When the laughter and commotion had subsided and the three were sipping leisurely at their drinks Greta Templeton looked at Faye and said with a dry, admiring gleam, 'Your Spanish is better than ours and we've been living in Spain for seven years. How do you do it?'

8

Faye smiled modestly. 'My grandmother was a Majorcan. I've been visiting the island since I was a child.' She didn't mind disclosing these details about herself. In the whole of the time since she had got to know the Templetons they had been content to chat about themselves, never once showing a desire to burden her with prying questions. It was because of this that she wanted to tell them a little about herself now. And anyway, she had to talk to someone about her good fortune, or explode.

Greta opened her blue eyes wide and exclaimed, 'Your grandmother! You don't look Spanish.'

'I'm not,' Faye laughed. 'My grandfather was very English. Doña Maria Lopez de Chalmers—to give her her full title—was his second wife.'

'Isn't it a small world!' Greta clapped her hands together with an expression of wonder and delight.

'Grandmother Chalmers was a marvellous old lady.' Faye reminisced smilingly. 'We used to come and visit her every summer. Her nursing home in Palma was like a hotel—she had her own suite and she would put us up there for a fortnight. Then Mum and Dad found they couldn't spare the time to leave the family business, so I've been driving down on my own these last three years.'

'Brave girl!' Greta said.

Faye shrugged, a soft light in her eyes. 'Doña Maria was in her nineties. She used to look forward to my visits. I couldn't possibly have disappointed her.'

'All the same, it's a gruelling drive,' Bart Templeton said, putting a fresh match to his pipe. 'I know, I've done it myself a few times.'

'True, it's hard going,' Faye admitted. And then with a dreamy look, 'But I won't have to worry about the drive down any more. This time I'm making a one-way trip.'

Greta tried not to look puzzled. 'But hasn't your

9

grandmother... ?'

'She died last year.' Faye took a sip of her drink. 'It was a surprise to us all ... the *finca*, I mean ... No one knew she had any property. Anyway,' Faye gulped and blurted out starry-eyed, 'she left it to me.'

'A real *finca*!' Greta clapped her hands again. In the same moment Faye fancied she saw the woman exchange looks with her husband before she went on, 'And now you're on your way to see what kind of a place it is you've inherited?'

'Well, more than that,' Faye explained happily. 'I'm going to live there.'

This time it seemed that husband and wife avoided each other's glances. 'Of course you've seen the property already?' Bart Templeton asked carefully.

'I've only just found out about it,' Faye laughed. 'I didn't want to have the bother of making two journeys, so I just packed up everything and here I am!'

'Well, that's wonderful!' Greta swivelled the cherry round in her drink and added thoughtfully, 'A *finca* is a kind of farm, isn't it? ... so it's bound to be a little bit rural....'

'I expect so,' Faye sighed blissfully. 'It's near a village called Caliséta. I found it on the map.'

'I know it.' Greta kept her eyes on her cherry stick. 'It's towards the centre of the island ... a little bit wild perhaps and....'

'And what?' Faye asked with a twinkle.

'Oh, it's a beautiful spot!' the woman confirmed hurriedly. 'It's just that ... well....' she shrugged weakly and tapered off.

'What Greta's trying to say,' Bart Templeton put in decisively, 'is that you might find country living in Majorca quite a bit different from the tourist spots and beaches around Palma.'

'Oh, I'll soon get the hang of it,' Faye replied happily.

'I expect you will.' Greta made an effort to sound enthusiastic. 'And what are your parents' views on this new life you've planned for yourself?'

'Oh, they think I'm slightly crazy,' Faye smiled, unperturbed. 'Especially as I haven't got a penny to my name.'

The laughter accompanying this remark was rather strained. Hardly noticing, Faye went on, dazzling them with her optimism, 'But I've got it all worked out. I'm going to paint.'

'Paint!' The couple echoed the word faintly.

'Yes. I'm an artist,' Faye said with a hint of pride in her sparkling gaze. 'I shall paint and sell my pictures to the tourists to make a living.'

The Templetons exchanged that look again. Their smiles were drooping at the edges. Greta looked about to make some comment, but whatever she had been going to say was cut off as her husband nudged her sharply and pointed out of the window. 'Well, what do you know! The lights of the island at last. Drink up, girls,' he picked up his glass, 'we'll be ashore in half an hour.'

There was a general commotion in the lounges as the passengers prepared for disembarkation. Pieces of luggage were being carefully counted and people with cabins went off to gather together their belongings. After eight hours afloat everyone was eager for action.

The waiters moved in to clear the empty glasses from the tables. Bart Templeton paid the bill. Rising with Faye to go, Greta said gaily, 'I've just had an idea! Why don't you come and put up with us for a night or two ... until you've had time to sort yourself out at the *finca*?'

'We're over at Porto Cristo,' her husband nodded, 'less than an hour's drive away from Caliséta. The hotel's closed, but you're welcome to a room on the house.'

'That's really very good of you both,' Faye smiled, taking the card that Greta pushed into her hand. 'But I think I'd like to get straight over to the house.' How could she explain to the couple that she had driven down from England in an agony of suspense, and that the long boat trip had been even more wearing on her nerves? Now that her journey was almost at an end she couldn't bear to wait a minute longer than was necessary to rush out and claim that which was her own.

'Well, just as you like. . . .' Greta wasn't very good at trying to sound off-hand. 'Only it's winter now, and the *finca*. . . .'

'What does that matter in Majorca?' Faye laughed. Hadn't she known only long golden days on the Mediterranean isle? 'I'm going to love every minute of it.'

A dubious silence greeted her remark as the couple walked with her across the carpeted spaces and out to the main stairway. Far too keyed up to notice it, Faye said politely, eager to be away, 'It's been lovely meeting you, and I *will* look you up when I get a minute. . . .'

'Yes, do,' the couple nodded. Then as Faye turned to take the stairs down to the car deck Greta stepped forward and called after her uncertainly, 'Are you sure you wouldn't rather. . . .'

' 'Bye! See you some time!' Faye broke away and waved cheerily. Half way down the steps she glanced back and saw the Templetons look at each other with helpless shrugs before moving off in the direction of their cabin.

All was activity below as the passengers with cars fussed and tinkered to make those last-minute adjustments. With a singing heart Faye hurried to join them. The lights of Palma were very close now. She took her place in the queue of vehicles her fingers itching on the driving wheel as the laboured throb of the ship's engines told her they were reversing in towards the shore.

What an age the business of docking seemed to take. The ship shuddered and rumbled as it moved into the side. The uniformed attendants hung about around the sealed hatchway as though reluctant to say goodbye to the lines of cars. Somewhere up top the ropes were secured; more shouting, and then at last the yawning hatch door was opened and fell to make a bridge for the madly revving machines.

It was after midnight before Faye's turn to drive off finally came. Wasting no time once she felt firm ground beneath her wheels, she swung away into the darkness past the maritime station buildings and the looming black shapes of other vessels in dock, and out on to the port road.

The rain which had accompanied the *San Carlo* on its trip from Barcelona was falling steadily. Faye had eyes only for the scene before her as she drove; one that she knew so well. The long ribbon of the Paseo Maritimo was garlanded with lights which were reflected in the sea, shimmering occasionally like a shower of restless stars. Eager to soak up all that was familiar to her, she drove on.

The cathedral was floodlit, its graceful spires piercing a sky streaked with the silver of a watery moon. Faye knew the Borne well and chose this avenue lined with magnificent chestnut trees to make her way up into the town. The rain could be seen slanting down in great sheets across the square where a fountain usually played. There were tourists in the gaily lit cafés, and taxis swished their way along the *calles*, but nobody ventured out on foot into the windswept night.

Driving carefully, Faye weaved her way along the narrow one-way streets and out into wide modern thoroughfares which brought her to the outskirts of the city, and to the main highway cutting across the island.

She found the route busier than she had expected

with most of the cars streaming in towards town as she slowly headed away from it. The sombre suburbs flanked the roadway in the form of shabby Majorcan terraced houses fronted by iron balconies, dimly-lit local cafés, tiny shuttered businesses and walled-off industrial blocks. Interspersing the drab faceless exteriors, like jewels set in clay, were new and shiny blocks of apartments.

Forging ahead, Faye gripped the driving wheel a little tighter. The rain hereabouts was quite startling. She had never seen anything like it. It drummed with jet force as it crashed down on the road in front of her, bouncing two or three inches high as it fell. She could see the steel rods of water illuminated in the headlights of slowly passing cars.

Out towards the open country conditions worsened. The road's surface disappeared beneath lakes of water; black, glistening stretches which were a nightmare to drive through. Several times Faye feared for the stability of her little car. Occasionally a lonely wayside restaurant, a-blur with lights and music to attract the ubiquitous tourist, swung by, but she had little time to let her gaze wander. She had covered some eighteen to twenty kilometres since starting out from Palma. Somewhere out this way was the turning off that would take her to Caliséta.

She had had plenty of opportunity to memorise the route from the map she carried with her and any time now there should be a hump-backed bridge coming up on the left . . . Yes, there it was! She could just make it out through the streaming windscreen. And a little further along on her right was the narrow opening she had been watching out for.

It was a relief to leave the main road behind with its continuous stream of headlights coming at her. At least there was little likelihood of her meeting similar night revellers returning home along a nondescript side lane

14

like this.

She travelled for some time through the impenetrable darkness. Then she began to have second thoughts about the lack of company. The road was narrow and winding, with nothing on either side but old stone boundary walls of fields and agricultural stretches. It snaked up slopes where clusters of pines roared in the wind and round bends where the rain gushed like a river.

Faye drove through these torrents nervously. They were deep enough to put her car out of action, and the last thing she wanted to do was find herself stranded out here. Sometimes when she came up round a high bend she would catch the glimpse of blurred lights of a town nestling far out on the distant plain, and occasionally a gleaming white villa would look down at her, smug and superior, from its dark pine-clad heights.

The rain was unceasing. It drummed on the car roof and streamed down the windscreen so that Faye almost missed the sign pointing to Caliséta. She backed up with difficulty and swung into the narrow turning. If the driving had been tedious before, it was now almost impossible. The road was unasphalted, and a sea of mud, churned up by the hooves of heaven knew what animals, shone wickedly in the headlights.

Pushed to its limits by the long drive down from England, the little Morris protested violently as its wheels sunk into the mire. Faye clung to the steering wheel and coaxed the car along, lurching from side to side. She knew that but for the fact that her father had paid for a new engine a couple of years ago, it would now be on the scrap heap.

She found Caliséta, a cluster of bulky old stone structures huddled together in the darkness at the side of the road. The road leading to San Mateo, the *finca*, was the first turning off after the village, and it couldn't come soon enough for Faye.

She was past being surprised at conditions now and when a rough side lane presented itself a little further along she swerved into it thankfully. What a drive it had been! She was worn out with the struggle of trying to keep afloat along the country roads. But she was almost home now, and a hot bath and bed was a blissful thought!

The track was very narrow. The car swayed sickeningly as it skidded over submerged rocks along the route, their surfaces polished by time to glass-like smoothness. Hastily Faye brushed steam from the windscreen. Despite the headlights she could see barely more than a yard ahead.

The track grew gradually narrower. The old stone walls on either side seemed to be closing in on her like pincers. She battled on, bumping and bouncing ahead, but when a fall of stones from one of the crumbling walls met her front wheels round a bend she knew she could drive no further.

Securing the brakes, she sat back in a mood of frustration. The raindrops spattered across the car bonnet and slanted viciously through the beams of the headlights. The heap of stones sat grinning maliciously in her path. Abruptly she switched off the headlights and groped for torch and umbrella. There was nothing for it but to go the rest of the way on foot. The house couldn't be far away now.

The freezing rain came as something of a shock to her. She locked the car door juggling with her lighted torch and spinning umbrella. How awful to have to step in all this mud! And the umbrella wasn't much use. It caught in the buffeting winds, making her slither and lose her balance so that several times she almost lost her torch in the darkness. Becoming more and more short-tempered with the antics of the wind, she snapped the umbrella down angrily—she was drenched anyway. She used it as a walking stick for a time, and to scrape some of the mud off her shoes, but in the end both she and it were in such a mess she tossed it away in disgust.

Her thick coat clung to her damply. She experienced bouts of cloying heat from the effort of trying to keep on her feet, and freezing cold as the wind clawed at her with icy fingers. How much further? Her spirits lifted when peering through the gloom she caught sight of a looming dark shape ahead. Thank heavens! San Mateo at last! It wouldn't be long now.

The track took her round in a series of annoying twists and turns. She was getting a better view of the building up ahead all the time. It looked colossal silhouetted against the rain-grey moon-blurred sky. Eventually she came to what appeared to be a walled in animal enclosure with stone shelters at the side. Pigs! Her nose wrinkled in distaste.

It was beginning to occur to her that the farm buildings looked terribly run down from what she could make out in this light. But even this reluctant observation didn't prepare her for the full view of the *finca* which met her round the final bend of the track.

Winged on one side by the cow byres and outbuildings and on the other by a decaying shell with a huge gaping hole which had once been a window, it stood back, a gaunt mass of stone with nothing to indicate at all that it might be a residence except the bleached and rotting sealed shutters and at its centre huge rustic double doors.

Standing in the spattering rain in the courtyard, for want of a better word, Faye stared at the desolate, cheerless and depressing hulk, all her rosy optimism evaporating with one glance. Was this then the property? *Her property* masquerading under the grand title of San Mateo? She couldn't believe it. And all the high hopes she had nursed of trellises and gardens and playing fountains and fruit trees!

Dejectedly she trudged up to the door. Well, she was here now, so there was little she could do about her disappointment. She needed warmth and dry clothes. Recalling that she had left her luggage locked in the car was enough to put the finishing touches to her gloom.

It came as a relief to find that she could push the big doors open, for she had no key. Walking with difficulty in her mud-caked shoes, she crept inside, and found herself in a bare stone-floored room. Her torch picked out one or two domestic oddments at the sides; bulging sacks, an old water pitcher, a toddler's pushchair. It seemed to be no more than an entrance parlour for a larger room beyond. Venturing through the opening, Faye was almost swallowed up in the vastness of the interior, its bareness relieved only by a heavy wooden trestle table covered with faded oilcloth, plus rough wooden chairs.

It was the corner to the right of the archway which held her attention. Here was an ingle-nook such as she had never seen before; a separate little stone-built enclosure dominated by the curved walls of a tremendous chimney, whitewashed and smoke-stained, which rose to the rafters above. The benches around the enclosure were covered with rough sheepskin rugs and there was a small table and chair in one corner.

Faye could feel a faint whisper of warmth as she stepped into the chimney nook. She was rather startled on swinging the torch away to see faint red embers among the log ash in the fireplace. She stepped back uneasily, a hand flying to her throat. How odd! As far as she knew, no one was expecting her.

A shiver passed through her, reminding her that she was tired, wet and cold. The stone-floored, barnlike interior was depressingly devoid of comfort. She found a door at the far end and opened it hopefully. There was an old-fashioned mahogany dining table and chairs in there and a glass-fronted cupboard showing a variety of crockery, but nothing resembling a bed. Another door opened on to a totally empty room.

Faye retraced her footsteps and groped her way back to the outdoors. There *must* be somewhere where she could lay her head for the night. Earlier she had noticed a flight of stone steps adjoining the house in the shadows on the left outside. She crept up these now, feeling even less confident than she had done rounding the lane on her arrival. Everything was so eerie, and there were the red embers in the hearth inside to be explained.

The steps took her up to a kind of anteroom projecting over the courtyard, which was the crumbling shell with the gaping hole in the side. But there was a rough wooden door in the wall adjoining the house. She pushed this open and slipped inside.

Immediately she sensed a difference about this part of the *finca*. The room she found herself in was of salon-like proportions with huge dark oil paintings hanging on the walls and old Regency-style couches, whose ancient upholstery one could imagine crumbling to dust at a touch, arranged beneath rotting drapes.

Muddy feet scuffing across the huge expanse of bare floor, Faye trained the beam of her torch first on one picture and then another, momentarily intrigued by the idea that here among these indistinct portraits might be the ancestors of her Spanish grandmother. For a while she forgot her discomfort. There was another door across from the main entrance, but she didn't give it a thought.

She was feeling the eeriness creep over her again as a ghostly face smiled out at her from the dark depths of a canvas when the door behind her was suddenly flung open and a man in smoking jacket, framed against the light streaming from within, asked angrily, 'May I ask what you are doing prowling around my house in the middle of the night?'

CHAPTER TWO

FAYE almost leapt into the air in fright. When she saw that the figure was no spectral form but normal flesh and blood, she felt a flood of guilt at being caught in the act like this. Then the guilt dispersed and hot on its tail came fury at being made to look a fool. How dare the man scare the wits out of her with his abrupt appearance? And what did he mean, *his house?*

Bedraggled, but nevertheless composed now she retorted witheringly, 'I beg your pardon! I'm not *prowling*. I am simply looking for a room in which to spend the night.'

'This is not a hotel,' the man replied irritably, 'and we don't cater for tourists who have lost their way.'

Faye's anger and indignation were now equal to his, especially as she caught a glimpse into the room behind him, carpeted and cheerfully lit, with a fire merrily blazing in the hearth. She drew herself up to all of her quivering five feet three and returned hotly, 'In that case might I ask what *you* are doing here?'

Their raised voices had started off a banshee howl down in the courtyard and quickly taking up the alert, the sounds of deep-throated barks, together with all kinds of baying, yowps, yelps and frantic yapping came drifting up the stairs. All designed, of course, Faye told herself crossly, to make her look like the interloper.

In the commotion a rustic-looking couple in night garb appeared at the top of the stairs in the doorway. The man, tousled and sleepy-eyed, held his lantern high and peered cautiously into the shadows. Faye ignored them completely and proceeded with the business of turning the squatter off her premises. 'Far from having lost my way, I am well aware of my whereabouts. And contrary to the opinion you appear to have on the subject, this is not *your* house. It's mine.'

The man framed in the lighted doorway obviously thought she was deranged. He removed his gaze distastefully from her wild, mud-smeared appearance and said in rapid Spanish to the night-robed couple, 'I've no idea what she's talking about, but give her a place to sleep for the night. I'll look into it in the morning.'

Faye, however, had no intention of being dismissed in this way. Going one better than his fluent Spanish, of which she had understood every word, she addressed the couple in pure Mallorquese. 'I would like a bedroom, if you please. And some hot water to get rid of these stains.' Then leaving the man in the smoking jacket to work *that* one out, she stalked out and down the steps after the shuffling couple.

She was shown into a room which was as cheerful as a monk's cell. Whitewashed throughout, the ceiling was concave and tapered upwards to cathedral-like heights over a brass-knobbed bedstead made up with bedding equally stark white in appearance. There was nothing else in the room.

It was just as well she had come empty-handed for the night Faye thought morosely, looking for a place to hang her soggy coat. The woman had disappeared, leaving the ancient lighting apparatus to illuminate the room fitfully with its stuttering flame. A few seconds later the night-garbed figure reappeared carrying an earthenware bowl of tepid water which she carefully placed in the middle of the floor. She smiled thinly as though she were offering all the amenities of the Ritz and stood rooted with shock when Faye asked if she might have a towel and some soap too.

Hastily closing the door when the woman had departed, Faye began to peel off her clothes. The water was freezing by the time she got to it. The draughty air, given full freedom in the tremendous amount of space in the room, struck every part of her as she hurriedly sluiced down.

Swathed in the towel, she hopped to the bed and slid between the sheets in her underwear. She had been lying for no more than a few seconds when a peculiar change came over her. At first she thought it must be her imagination. But no! Slowly, insidiously a cold penetrating clamminess began to make itself felt on her person. Shivering, she turned over and curled up tight like a ball. That didn't help. The tighter she curled the more her skin and clothes began to ooze like moss soaked in early morning dew. She searched for warmth and sleep and found neither. In the end, after gritting her teeth for ten minutes, she clawed her way frustratedly out of the covers. The bed was damp! It must have been made up like this for months, maybe years! Crossly she groped about in the dark. To combat pneumonia she dressed again in her woollen sweater and thick skirt, then wearily climbed back into bed.

Once she was under the covers the effect was now one of a Turkish bath. She punched the pillow and curled up resignedly. Well, at least now it was warm damp! As she lay there trying to relax she thought fumingly of the man upstairs enjoying all the comforts of a mansion. Who was he? And what was he doing at San Mateo? He was English, of course, as his opening remark to her in the shadows of the vast salon had shown.

Gloweringly she recalled his superior manner and his tone of address as though she had been some petty pilferer creeping about. She tugged the bedcovers up around her chin. His house indeed! Well, they would soon see about that! Past caring about the all-enveloping damp, she fell asleep.

It was still dark when all manner of unmusical sounds came to invade her unconsciousness. Distant thumps and faint shouts could be heard above the hysterical squabbling of poultry, noisy hammering and clang-clang of bells. The smell of horses drifted under Faye's nose. She stuck it into the pillow and dozed. A voice from somewhere in the house shook the foundations with its volume. '*Anofre! No dues se lena?* Anofre! Haven't you got that firewood yet?' Faye began to wish she didn't understand the coarse peasant language quite so well.

She clung stubbornly to the mists of sleep, angrily pulling the covers over her head and the pillow around her ears. Domestic goings-on at the crack of dawn was all she needed! Her determination to sleep on must have paid off, for she was wrapped blissfully in a cocoon of warmth and slumber when a terrific hammering came from close at hand.

Peevishly she opened her eyes. There was a slab of grey sky showing through a window high up in the wall. The thumping, she discovered, was somebody's fist battering on the door. 'Well, come in, it's open!' Faye called out exasperatedly.

Clumsily a figure appeared. It was the woman of last night and the owner of the firewood clarion call of earlier. Her staring eyes fixed on Faye were full of the avid curiosity and fierce bewilderment of last night as she said accusingly, 'The *guardia civil* are outside. They want to see you.'

'To see me? Whatever for?' Faye sat up foggily.

'I don't know.' The woman gripped her forearms across her middle as though hoping for the worst. 'But you're to come right away.' With a hostile look on her face she clumped away.

Faye tumbled out of bed on to the stone floor. Frantically brushing the creases from her skirt and sweater, she hopped about looking for her shoes. What on earth did the *guardia civil* want with her? She had met many of these young uniformed law-officers in their official capacity at the ports and on the roads throughout Spain and had always found them courteous and polite. She couldn't think what she had done to upset the local contingent. Hoping they wouldn't notice her muddy shoes, she hurried out.

Outside was like a stage set with everybody waiting for her arrival. In the grey morning, surrounded by pecking hens, snuffling piglets and barking dogs, the Majorcan couple stood and watched her appearance as though they fully expected justice to be done. The two *guardia civil* in their olive-green uniforms and black patent leather hats were chatting beside their scooters at the end of the lane. Close to them in the courtyard she spotted the man from upstairs. Dressed in a grey suit, he stood eyeing her approach contemplatively, with one foot resting on the running board of an expensive car.

His deep-set gaze showed a flicker of interest now that she had washed the mud off. Well, let him look all he liked! Airily Faye flaunted her mane of red-gold hair, her smooth features set and wide-set hazel eyes glinting. She caught the glimpse of a firm jaw and a mouth clamped tight over suppressed humour, but she had no intention of returning the man's scrutiny.

She stalked on towards the *guardia civil* and almost fell headlong over a flock of turkeys who were just rounding the corner from the lane. As surprised as she was at the encounter, they hissed and blew themselves up menacingly, strutting and thumping their annoyance before retreating on flapping wings with high-pitched bursts of idiotic laughter. Startled out of her wits, she marched on, a little pinker in the face, towards the uniformed officials.

She wondered anxiously what terrible crime she had committed; although to look at the two men there seemed scant cause for concern. They were smiling broadly, and being youthful and truly Spanish, they were more interested in her mode of approach than they were in rushing to the business in hand.

The one with the moustache and engaging gap in his smile saluted her smartly on her arrival. '*Buenas dias, señorita.*' He held up a muddy truncheon-like object. 'Does this belong to you?'

Faye stared at her umbrella, grubby and still wet with rain. 'Why, yes....' she stammered. 'I ... er ... lost it in the lane last night.'

The other *guardia civil,* making an effort to appear serious while probing her golden gaze with his flashing dark eyes, continued with the formalities. 'During our inspection of the roads in the neighbourhood this morning we came upon an abandoned car in a disused *camino*. As there was no one around, only this....' he grinned at the soggy umbrella.

Oh, the car! So that's why they were here! Faye breathed an inward sigh of relief. 'It's mine, I'm afraid,' she admitted lamely. 'I had to leave it last night....' With that superior presence standing beside his car in the background she explained how she had got into driving difficulties, hoping that the man noted well her fluency in Spanish.

'So it is clear!' came the jovial comment. 'You lost your way.'

'I most certainly did not,' Faye corrected coldly. 'I knew perfectly well I was making for San Mateo.'

'But the *finca* ...' the men fidgeted and cast embarrassed smiles towards the gleaming car behind them, 'it is the residence of Señor Garrett.'

Faye shot a frosty glance in the same direction and caught the glimpse of an amused light. She tossed her hair back from her shoulders haughtily. She couldn't see what was so funny. In crisp tones she said, 'Contrary to public opinion, gentlemen, *I* am the owner of this property. I have come out from England and I intend to make my home here.'

The *guardia civil* eyed her up and down, then transferred their glances to the other car. Said the one with the moustache, slanting the man a wicked grin, 'You have an interesting problem on your hands, Señor Garrett.'

Some lazy comment was made, but Faye couldn't catch what it was because of the noisy revving-up of the scooters. She didn't, however, miss the satirical white smile accompanying the man's reply, which only served to increase her annoyance.

Astride their machine the *guardia civil* beckoned her cheerfully to follow. They told her above the din of their chattering engines, 'You took the wrong turning last night. The old track from the village is no longer in use. Come, you will need some assistance with your car.'

Swerving away, they turned their glances back to her encouragingly. Seeing that she had no choice in the matter Faye started out on foot behind them. They went at a snail's pace so as not to leave her too far behind, and took the lane which skirted the farm buildings. This route was rock-free and level, with a sandy surface, and she could see the main road only a few yards ahead.

From behind her she could hear the hiss of car tyres on the rainy wet surface, and knew that it was the self-assured Señor Garrett at the wheel, in her footsteps. Obviously he had been waiting for the scooters to move off so that he too could drive out. Well, he had only to ask if he wanted to pass. And if he made no sign *she* certainly wasn't going to get out of his way. If he was hoping to unnerve her with his presence at the rear he was in for a disappointment. She could well imagine the ghost of that satirical light still in his eyes as he hounded her playfully from behind. Well, he was welcome to his own amusements!

She strolled on, but try as she might to appear unaffected at the sound of his car tyres brushing her skirts, her legs soon began to feel as though they didn't belong to her; they did silly things over which she had no control. She tripped and stumbled over the smallest pebble, but always regained her balance with poker-straight back and head flung high to hide her feeling of foolishness. And hair flaming out behind, hips swinging purposefully, she marched on.

At the main road the scooters turned left in the direction of the village, and it was with quivering relief that Faye watched the gleaming car turn away to the right. Nothing would induce her, of course, to look the man's way as his hand came out in a salute of farewell to the *guardia civil*. His deep voice laced with irony called, '*Adios, amigos*. Best of luck with the chariot hunting!'

He slid away smoothly in *his* expensive 'chariot' and Faye, glad to see the back of him, followed the waving men on their machines.

She soon saw that if she had driven a little further along the main road last night she would have come to the true entrance to San Mateo, for only a short distance down the road the men were swerving into the rocky lane that she had taken in her hurry to avoid the rain.

The scooters bucked and bounced over the stones, arriving only a few minutes ahead of her at the scene of her grimy, battered little Morris caught like a fly in a web among the heap of rubble. She produced the car keys and gallantly the men set to work, one at the wheel and the other one shouting the orders at the rear as the vehicle was backed out towards the road.

Beaming broadly and enjoying the whole thing, the uniformed men worked enthusiastically, taking suicidal risks with the nonchalance of small boys walking in front of an express train. Miraculously they got the car out on to the road without a scratch to themselves or the machine, though Faye felt slightly limp merely from watching!

With a flourish the men invited her to take the wheel and once she was behind it they escorted her with all the pageantry of royalty back up the main road, round on to the sandy stretch of lane and eventually into the courtyard of San Mateo.

Faye waved as with a joint *'Buenos dias, señorita,'* they slid gallantly away, but once they were out of sight her lips clamped into an angry line, and she marched towards the house. The first job was to sort out this Señor Garrett!

In the doorway, the Majorcan couple were standing with folded arms as though they were determined to assert the Englishman's rights. Faye had had quite enough of this. 'I'd like some breakfast, please, and a hot drink.'

The woman gaped. 'Breakfast?' she queried stupidly.

'Si, desayuno,' Faye emphasised briskly. 'And coffee if you have it.'

'Coffee there is,' came the sullen reply, *'pero. . . .'*

Faye ignored the negative response. 'Bring me something to eat,' she said crisply, moving towards the car. Breakfast might be an unheard-of luxury in this part of Spain, but she was determined to have some.

A thin drizzle came on while she was unloading her luggage. She made several trips through the house to the room she had occupied last night, although this was merely a temporary arrangement as far as she was concerned. She struggled with her suitcases and battled with her easel and painting materials and when everything was inside she searched out something dry to wear.

A few minutes later she was still bathed in discomfort. It was odd. Though she had changed every item of her clothing she still had a wet chill on her skin; the wretched damp seemed to percolate into everything. Even the sealed car and her locked suitcases had been no match for its insidious presence. In a depressed state Faye went in search of food.

On the long trestle table in the main room she found a sight which did little to cheer her. Cut from a huge round loaf, two slices of bread flapped over the edges of a mammoth dinner plate. Olive oil had been poured liberally over them, and dotting each one were chunks of the cooking tomatoes of which Majorcans were so fond, and which hung in strings by the door.

Repelled by the sickly-sweet odour of oil, Faye carried the plate into the chimney-nook. At least the roaring fire which blazed in the grate was a blessing. The bread was totally unsatisfying because it had no salt in it; the tomatoes, however, were delicious, and somehow she managed to wade through enough of the whale-sized slices to take the edge off her hunger.

The drizzle had settled into a steady downpour by the time Faye had freshened up in her room. She donned a raincoat and made a dash for the car and reached it only half soaked. Letting in the clutch, she swung away, wondering if she would ever feel dry again.

Leaving Caliséta behind, she swished through the sheets of water which threatened to flood her engine at every turn, wondering bleakly if anyone had ever heard of road drainage in these parts. The way ahead was just a grey wall of mist and rain, but she swung the wheel determinedly. She knew well enough where she was going.

In all there were three or four biggish towns on the island, excluding the city of Palma. Llosaya, the nearest one to San Mateo, was where the executors of her grandmother's estate had their offices. A certain José Andrés Moreno had written to her in England, and Faye couldn't wait to have a word with him now.

After about twenty minutes' driving she came into the outskirts of the town; streets of flat-topped terraced houses, their tightly shuttered windows and doors giving them a deserted look. In the centre of Llosaya where giant chestnut trees dripped steadily the rain didn't dampen the animation of the shoppers who stood in the garlic- and sausage-festooned doorways chattering happily while waiting to be served.

Faye found the lawyer's offices in a big corner building topped by a bell tower, its front ornately carved.

Don José Andrés was a square man with short white hair and drooping bloodhound features which almost met up with his round, distended middle. In his dusty business suit he greeted Faye profusely, a smile lighting up his sad features. 'My dear Miss Chalmers! I had no idea you were on the island.'

She was offered a chair, after which she wasted no time in getting down to straight talk.

'Señor Moreno, it's true, is it not, that my grandmother left the *finca* at Caliséta to me?'

'It is true indeed,' came the smiling reply.

'Then why is it,' Faye pursued indignantly, 'that when I arrived late last night and went in search of a room to sleep I was confronted by a man who accused *me* of trespassing?'

'Ah yes! Señor Garrett.' Don José put his finger-tips together with a meditative gleam.

Faye bit back her exasperation. If anyone else mentioned that man's name she was sure she would do something drastic!

The lawyer looked at her enquiringly. 'You say you arrived last night. May I ask the reason for your visit?'

'Of course,' Faye made an effort not to sound short. 'When I received your letter telling me of my grandmother's bequest, I decided there and then to make San Mateo my home. And so that there should be no doubts on the matter,' she added, 'it's my intention to live permanently at the *finca*.'

'I see.' José Andrés sat back in his rocking chair. He had short legs one of which he tucked up behind the other. With the one foot he rocked vigorously, almost lost beneath his paunch. At last he spoke. 'San Mateo was once a vast mansion with huge salons,' he told Faye. 'Today very little of its former grandeur remains. The Rodriguez couple do their best to farm the property, but labour being what it is these days the place is sadly run down. However, it has always been our policy to do what we can with the estates we handle.'

Here it comes, thought Faye, itching for the man to get on with it. He rummaged through the papers on his desk and finding nothing went on, 'Brent Garrett is designing a golf course in the neighbourhood, a few miles from the village of Caliséta. He wanted somewhere close by where he could work. As you will understand, we knew nothing of your impending arrival, so when Mr Garrett came to us—we run a small estate agency on the premises—' José Andrés smiled puckishly—'we agreed to let him have the west wing of San Mateo on a rental basis.'

Faye was on her feet instantly. 'But that is totally unacceptable to me,' she protested, 'I want him out.'

'That, I am afraid, Miss Chalmers, will not be possible,' came the careful reply. 'All the papers have been signed for a stay of one year. Señor Garrett took up residence four weeks ago. That gives him an eleven-month tenancy over which neither you nor I have any control.'

Faye sat down, stunned and deflated.

While she was recovering from the shock of what she had just heard, José Andrés viewed her ponderingly and said with a sly gleam in his eyes, 'You are feeling a little disappointed with your legacy, no? The *finca* is, after all, in an appalling state of neglect.'

'Naturally I expected something a bit grander,' Faye admitted gloomily.

'Cheer up, things are not as bad as they seem.' The sly gleam still very much in evidence, the lawyer delved into a drawer at the side of his desk and came up with a sheaf of papers. He flicked over the top one and said casually, 'San Mateo is one of the few large farming estates which have remained in production for its almond and carob harvest. Did you know that the land belonging to the *finca* amounts to several thousand acres?'

'Well, no, I didn't,' Faye stammered. She had been mainly concerned with having a roof over her head.

'Knowing the value of land these days, I would say, Señorita Chalmers, that you could be a very rich woman indeed.' José Andrés gave her his careful smile. Then he took to rocking vigorously in his chair again. 'My letter to you didn't cover all the aspects of your late grandmother's will. As there are certain conditions attached I thought it best first to familiarise you with your position before bringing in the points mentioned. However, now that you are here, there is no reason why you shouldn't know all the facts concerning yourself and San Mateo.'

Faye felt an ominous chill steal over her as she tried to unravel José Andrés' legal talk. What *conditions* was he talking about? And what had he meant when he had said she *could* be a very rich woman indeed?

The lawyer meandered pleasantly, 'Doña Maria Lopez de Chalmers was your grandfather's second wife, I believe?'

'That's right.' Faye felt obliged to fill him in on the details, though she was bursting to hear what he had to tell her. 'My father and his younger brother were very small when my widowed grandfather met Señora Lopez. She was in service in a small seaside hotel where the family used to stay.'

'They married consequently, I believe, and had many happy years together.'

'Over forty years,' Faye confirmed. 'As Grandfather's wife, Doña Maria became mother and grandmother to us all.'

'And she returned to the island sixteen years ago when your grandfather died.' The lawyer went back to scanning the papers in front of him.

'Yes.'

As though he sensed the impatience in her José Andrés looked long and hard at her. Then he tossed the papers to one side, leaned back in his chair and said smilingly, 'Well, it's all very simple. In view of the happy years she spent as the wife of an Englishman, your grandmother's expressed wish was that you should benefit from the same experience. In reverse, of course.'

'That *I* should benefit from the same experience?' Faye mouthed the words, staring at him idiotically.

Perhaps realising that it did no good to wrap his sentences in a protective legal coating, José Andrés leaned forward and said with quixotic forthrightness, 'To put it another way, Señorita Chalmers, it was Doña Maria's express desire that you should marry a Spaniard within two years of inheriting San Mateo.'

Faye's mouth dropped open. For several moments she was speechless. Then as the implications began to trickle through to her numbed brain she protested in embarrassment, 'Get married? But I've never given such a thing a thought ... and in any case....' As another thought crossed her mind she stopped her flustered expostulations and looked at the lawyer. 'What happens if I don't? Marry a Spaniard, I mean,' she asked faintly.

'The property together with all the land entailed is to be turned over to the state.'

Winded, Faye dropped back in her chair. She said eventually with a dazed, wry gleam, 'Doña Maria de Lopez must really have had a ball being married to my grandfather.'

José Andrés smiled, encouraged by her dry humour. He returned the papers to his drawer and told her with

33

fatherly consideration, 'None of this need concern you now. There is nothing to stop you doing as you please at San Mateo. But no actual cash benefits derived from the estate can be paid to you until the day of your marriage.'

He rose in his expansive manner, and realising, in a stunned way, that the interview was at an end, Faye got to her feet. With the courteousness of the Spaniard José Andrés bowed, kissed her hand, and rushed on his short legs to open the door for her. She gave him a watery smile of farewell and groped her way to the outdoors. She felt stunned by the events of the morning.

It wasn't so much the thought of her grandmother's dying request which sapped the strength from her legs, although that was shattering enough. What made her seethe with resentment and almost tearful frustration was the fact that she was stuck with the irksome Brent Garrett. Complete with his oozing self-assurance and satirical smile, he was a fixture on her property. And there wasn't a thing she could do about it!

CHAPTER THREE

IN the pouring rain Faye trudged towards her car. She just had to sit down and think things out. Life had been nothing but shocks since she had arrived in Majorca. She needed time to adjust herself to this new situation which had suddenly been thrust upon her, and she slid into the driving-seat with a relieved sigh.

How different it all seemed now from her rosy dreams of only a few days ago. The *finca* in which she had pictured herself living in grand style was little more than an ancient ruin. And even her complete ownership of that was tantalisingly in the balance, depending on whether or not she married a Spaniard before she was twenty-four.

But two years was a long time, she told herself practically. She needn't bother her head about that for the moment. No, the prickly problem was Brent Garrett. Not only did he possess a tenancy for eleven months more at San Mateo—after which time his precious golf course would be finished, one presumed—but he was living in the most habitable part of the house. The west wing, as José Andrés had called it, possessed a kind of faded old-world elegance which even in its crumbling, dusty state suggested comfort of a sort.

Morosely, she watched a group of children straggling through the rain outside. The weather didn't seem to bother them at all. They laughed and dragged each other through the mud, holding their faces to the raindrops as though they had all the time in the world to get home to Mother. This, coupled with the sight of a white donkey pulling a spindly tall-wheeled cart and a man with skin as wrinkled and brown as his corduroy clothing, heartened Faye a little. Gradually as she watched the passage of people outside, she began to feel her spirits lighten. She was here in Spain! Wasn't that enough to start with? How could she expect everything to run smooth from the first moment? This was a big step she was taking, starting life anew out here. Naturally she would have to learn to cope with the difficulties that presented themselves at the outset.

All at once Faye felt full of fight again. What if this Brent Garrett *was* living at San Mateo? There was always the farmhouse, wasn't there? And for the time being the *finca* was her property. As José Andrés had said, she could do as she pleased there.

Why shouldn't she go ahead exactly as she had planned? She was the mistress of San Mateo, Brent Garrett was merely a tenant. He needn't think his presence in the west wing was going to make the slightest bit of difference to *her*.

35

With vigour she started the car, almost sending the wheels on to the pavement in her new assertive mood. Now more than ever she felt ready to do battle in claiming the *finca* as her own. As for the Spanish husband, she'd find a way round that obstacle when she got to it.

She looked at the dismal day with new eyes. This was Majorca, her favourite island, and she was going to enjoy every minute of her new life here to the full.

All drive now, she planned her day. First she would shop for food. The sickly memory of the oil-soaked bread at the farmhouse put this at the top of her list. Then while she was here in Llosaya she would get to know the town and find out what amenities it offered for the tourists. This information would prove useful to her later, especially when she wanted to sell her paintings. Afterwards she would return to San Mateo and get herself organised for living!

It was well into the afternoon when Faye finally took the road out of town leading to Caliséta. Though still fired with determination she drove with a shade less bounce than when she had first started out after making the new pact with herself. The prices of food at the supermarket had come as rather a shock, and she looked at the small pile of groceries on the seat beside her and thought of the deep hole they had made in her purse. The money she had scraped together to take her over the first few weeks of settling in would go absolutely nowhere at this rate!

Worse, the display amenities in the town for artists' pictures had been disappointing. There were one or two showrooms and exhibition centres, if one was willing to overlook the fact that they were no more than converted stables and disused winery sheds. However, an attendant keeping an eye on a paltry collection of pictures in one of these establishments had told her

36

that little effort was made to attract buyers at this time of the year, but in the summer there was much more scope for selling one's work. Faye had had to be satisfied with this, and really when she thought about it now it was much to her advantage. At least it would give her time to get a stock of paintings ready.

Resolutely she swung round into the road leading to San Mateo, and with a flourish she came to a halt a few seconds later in the courtyard. As she parked the car it gave her immeasurable satisfaction to see Brent Garrett's sleek, precision-built machine as grimy and as mud-streaked as her own. With a nonchalant air she gathered up her groceries, and pointedly ignoring the flight of steps and the left wing, she made her way into the farmhouse.

In the communal kitchen an iron cauldron was simmering away above the coals in the chimney nook. The trestle table was set out with dark earthenware bowls and cutlery. Because there was nowhere else available Faye took her provisions to the small table beside the fire in the chimney nook. How welcome was the warmth! Out in the rain all morning she had grown almost numb with cold. With a grateful sigh she peeled off her damp outdoor garments and sat down to toast herself in the glow.

The Rodriguez woman came in. They had never been formally introduced, so Faye had no idea how to approach her; not, she was thinking, that she would have had much success, for the woman still circled her as though sticking to the old adage *If you ignore it, it will go away.* There was, however, less hostility in her manner and when she had stirred the mess in the pot over the flames and made several excursions to and from the trestle table, she looked at Faye with her wild staring eyes and said, 'I've set a place for you at the table.'

'Thank you, but I've just eaten,' Faye lied smilingly.

She had actually been nibbling biscuits and fruit on the drive back from town and the sight of the floating globules of fat in the cauldron defeated any appetite she might have had left over.

The Majorcan woman obviously had her suspicions. She eyed the packeted supermarket provisions on the table as if it was the stuff they fed ailing chicks on, and said, 'Good wholesome farm food is what you need. You're too thin.'

Faye broadened her smile and said nothing. How well she knew from her grandmother that the fashion on the island was to eat and eat and eat, and any girl who didn't waddle around under rolls of fat was regarded as an object of pity by the rest of the community. However, that was local fashion. Faye was quite content to keep her curves as they were, but she knew there was no point in trying to explain this. And it was nice to know that she had stirred that much interest in the woman's bosom. As a further gesture towards peaceful relations Faye offered to help in bringing the bowls from the trestle table so that the contents of the cauldron could be ladled in.

The other diners came in from the outside. There was the farm woman's husband, the famed Anofre of the firewood call, wearing an old sack cape-wise over his rough farm clothes as protection against the rain. He tossed this into a corner and trudged to warm his hands at the fire. As he glanced round from the flames his face was split by a grin which Faye hadn't seen before. His mouth was no more than a dark gap with one or two brown pegs faintly visible. In his black beret she could guess that he had been a handsome man before the years of sun and wind had taken its toll, criss-crossing his features with deep lines and weathering his skin so that it resembled the warm russet-red of a withered apple. He didn't say a word as he looked at Faye, but his face wore an expression of

bucolic good humour and mingling with the be-
wildered look in his eyes which seemed to be part of
the country make-up was a facetious twinkle. The
other two men, farm labourers, who had come in were
similar in dress and appearance and eventually all sat
down to the steaming bowls at the trestle table.

Warm, if not very comfortable, on her upright chair
in the ingle-nook, Faye faced the fire and tried to make
herself look invisible, reluctant to move out into the
draughty spaces beyond the chimney enclosure. So
weary after a bad night and a hectic morning, she could
have dozed and perhaps would have done but for the
noises being made at the trestle table.

Faye kept telling herself blithely that she was not in
the least affected by these wallowing noises. But then
her stomach began to protest in such a way that she
was obliged to make herself into a shadow and slip
silently away. It seemed a good idea at that time to do
some unpacking in her room.

When she arrived there she found the bed made up
in its white shrouds and the rest of the room wearing
its original bare look. The whereabouts of her suitcases
and all her clothes was a mystery for a while, until she
discovered a low cupboard flush with the wall on the
far side of the bed. Everything of hers had been stuffed
away in there as though the fewer reminders there were
of her presence, the better.

Patiently Faye dragged out her possessions once again
and laid everything out on the bed. There seemed to
be nowhere else, which brought her round to the question of a wardrobe of some kind. It was no use looking
for more secret hideaways in the walls, for the room
had the austere dimensions of a monastery cloister.
Outside she looked thoughtfully down the passageway.
Perhaps there would be something in one of the other
rooms. It was worth a try.

Everything was whitewashed and all angles and

curves as she moved over the undulating levels of polished stone. The tremendous thickness of the walls could easily be seen in the tiny window openings, showing bleak stretches of rubbled terrace and rain-shrouded countryside. There was no glass, or window-frames in the openings. Faye shivered. She was already feeling wretchedly cold away from the fire in the kitchen.

She found the door to a room a few yards along from that of her own. Her nose wrinkled at the sickly sweet odour permeating through every crack, and she pondered on whether to go in. The Rodriguez couple didn't sleep down this way or she would have heard them last night; therefore it was fairly safe to assume that these were spare bedrooms. She needed furniture for her room, so why shouldn't she winkle it out for herself? Who could say? She might come upon a nice antique wardrobe or a good solidly-built dressing table.

Eagerly she turned the knob. Nothing happened. The door opened a fraction, but there was something behind it. The strong-scented mustiness came at her in waves now. Far too determined to give up at this stage, she heaved and strained and pushed, feeling the door give an inch at a time. When it was opened wide enough she stuck her head inside.

The sight which met her eyes floored her completely. The interior was about the same size as the room she was sleeping in. Opposite the door was a square window opening such as she had seen coming along the passageway, and the cold air constantly wafting through was doing a nice job of keeping the contents aired. A waist-high sea of carob beans!

Brown and dusty like a lot of flattened, shrivelled bananas, they covered the entire expanse of floor and rose up the walls to a depth which almost reached the window. Faye stared, holding her nose at the powerful, aromatic fumes. Now she knew why she hadn't been able to open the door. The room was full of horse fodder!

There were two more doors towards the end of the passageway. Intrigued now, she had to know what was behind them. Having been forewarned she opened the first one and hardly batted an eyelid at the sight of the straw-strewn floor. There was a corner fireplace with an empty dusty wine bottle on the hob. A rusting petrol drum stood nearby, and on the opposite side beneath an open loft was the rotting remains of an old farm cart. Rustic double-doors beyond the cart suggested a barn-cum-living room.

Hastily Faye moved on. The last door was the biggest surprise of the lot. It opened on to no more than a brick enclosure, with a low rattan roof and huge earthenware bowls cemented into porthole openings in the outer walls. Half of each shallow bowl projected out into the open and Faye suspected that it was from outside that food was fed to whatever happened to be cooped up in here at the time. The proximity of farm animals was pungently obvious, and judging by the height of the bowls from the floor, pigs, she fancied, were the most likely guests here!

Believing now that there could be no more shocks, Faye made for the outer door at the end of the passageway. Here at least was a pleasant surprise. It opened on to a strip of grassy terrace which was turning a deep lush green under the pattering rain. Six feet or more below this terrace, a short space from the doorway, was a similar grassy strip and stretching far out into the distance, parallel with the stepped terraces, was a rolling valley. Faye's interest revived. She had had no idea that the *finca* was perched on a hillside.

Eagerly she turned left outside the doorway with the intention of taking a few steps alongside the great walls of the house, and in doing so came face to face with a huge black and white cow.

41

The horned lady's astonishment was clearly no less than Faye's although as she jerked up her head, her bovine expression remained unaltered. Placid or not, she looked as though she might charge at any moment. Backing off slowly, then speeding up her retreat, Faye turned and fled into the house, falling against the door as she frantically slammed it shut behind her. As though to add the finishing touches to her hair-raising tour a pair of grey and white doves fluttered up in panic from somewhere above her head and settled down again amidst a gurgle of indignant coos.

In sour mood Faye retraced her steps along the passageway. She had a whitewashed room, a bed and a cupboard, and she was at least ten seconds' walk away from the nearest livestock. What did she have to complain about?

Once back in the comparative sanctuary of her own room she set about the business of dealing with her clothes. Their dewy look worried her, but she was not surprised at the state they were in. With everything going drip-drip around here and no indoor heat to offset the damp, it was clear that they were gathering more moisture from the air all the time they lay out in the open. And there was no question of folding them away in this condition.

The kitchen fire seemed to be the only source of heat in the place, so—Faye gathered up a bundle and marched out determinedly. For a start she meant to have the comfort of dry clothes!

As it happened her belligerent mood was unnecessary. The communal kitchen was deserted. The trestle table had been cleared and its oilcloth wiped down. Everyone, it seemed, had returned to their work around the farm. Briskly, Faye pulled the chairs out from the table and one by one arranged them around the fire.

With the house to herself she had a high old time

airing out her clothes. Where did all the moisture come from? Her woollies positively steamed before the flames; skirts and slacks smoked a little too. She worked in relays between the fire in the chimney nook and her room; when one batch was warm and fleecy and folded again, she transferred it to the wall cupboard before bringing out another lot.

Completely absorbed in her task, she had just rounded up the last of the odds and ends and strung everything out over the chairs when a footstep sounded through the archway from outside and a voice called out sharply, 'Ana! Is Ana there?'

Rooted, Faye watched as a masculine figure strode into view. Then, with flame-red cheeks, she lunged at the clothes around the fire, grabbing at the panties, underslips and bras which festooned the chairs, and stuffed them anywhere so long as they were out of sight.

She was quick, but not quick enough, judging by the irritating glint of humour in the blue eyes which now openly surveyed her. Obviously forgetting his previous quest for the moment, he relaxed his frame to the point of being sardonic and moved into the room. Faye could tell by his expression that he too had made a hasty visit to Llosaya to consult with José Andrés on the business of his renting the west wing of the *finca*. That he knew the strength of his position was odiously apparent in his manner. Swaggeringly self-assured, his hands thrust casually in his pockets, he said in English, in the clear-cut tones of the southerner, 'My name's Brent Garrett.'

'I know. You wouldn't consider vacating your rooms by the end of the week, would you?'

Faye's blunt approach had no effect on the man. He ignored her rebuff and went on lazily, 'And yours is Faye Chalmers. The name doesn't suit you somehow.' He eyed her warlike expression with a cryptic gleam.

'Although you've improved a bit since I first saw you last night.'

'Well, thanks!' Faye replied drily. She began folding the least revealing of her undergarments for the simple reason that she found it distinctly unnerving just standing there with his mocking blue gaze trailing over her.

Last night he had been ready to throttle the life out of her on her arrival, believing her to be some mud-spattered prowling night-thief. Now he appeared to regard the whole thing as a joke. Well, of course he could afford to smile, she mused acidly, *he* had the best part of the house.

Insufferably sure of himself, he suggested with laconic humour, 'As we're both going to reside under the same roof, maybe we should sit down and have a nice cosy discussion on each other's living habits?'

'If you don't mind, I've got things to do.' Faye flapped a frilly underslip under his nose.

'Just as you say.' Brent Garrett shrugged easily and moved off, slanting her a mocking grin as he went. 'Just trying to promote harmonious relations....'

Hmmmph! Faye watched him go, hearing him take up his call for the elusive Ana once he was out of sight. Funny man! She flapped another garment, making it crack in the air for his benefit, but as her gaze lingered on the now deserted archway a flicker of humour tugged at the sullen droop of her lips.

Mechanically she went on folding her clothes, while her mind toyed with the picture of the man she had just seen. He had brown hair to go with his blue eyes. She noticed that he wore it parted at the side and that it was cut in such a way that it grew thickly over his neatly shaped head without hanging down untidily. His nose was sharpish but somehow it suited his face, which could be described as ruggedly handsome. He was wearing a daffodil-yellow sweater over a chocolate-brown woollen knit shirt and slacks and the effect when

44

he smiled had been a little earth-shaking.

Waking up abruptly, Faye shook out any garment she could lay her hands on to dispel the vision which was threatening to put a stop to her activities. As if she was remotely interested in what her lodger looked like!

Around tea-time Faye's mind turned towards the subject of food. Spanish mealtimes were totally different from the ones she had been used to. Over here they made do with just a drink for breakfast; had a tremendous meal about three o'clock in the afternoon and another around nine or ten o'clock at night.

With her stomach rumbling the way it was, she obviously couldn't wait until almost bedtime to eat. The problem was how did she go about preparing herself a meal of something like eggs and bacon and perhaps fried mushrooms, and a pot of tea with a great cauldron of greasy water simmering over the fire? She sat and figured it out and decided that even though they might be no less primitive, there must be some kind of alternative cooking arrangements in some other part of the farmhouse.

The thought of what she might find as she set off on a search filled her with a mixture of fascination and dread. It didn't take her long to discover what she was looking for. The Majorcan woman, who she now knew went by the name of Ana, had brought coffee in from the outdoors this morning, so the outdoors seemed the logical place to start with.

Faye had prepared herself for the worst, but even her vivid imagination couldn't do justice to what she found. Across the courtyard, facing the farmhouse doorway, was a tumbledown stone-built hut. A trail of blue smoke drifting upwards from the length of drainpipe sticking up from the flat roof, which could be described as a chimney, beckoned Faye forward. Hypnotised, she ignored the tethered yelping dogs who were taking their time in accepting her presence around the *finca*, and moved towards the low doorway.

The rough interior reminded her of an outside coalhouse in England, although there was little enough space inside to liken it to anything. A wide bench filled the whole of one side, and was cluttered with every conceivable object relating to household lumber; old shoes, plastic bottles of cleaning liquid, fragments of horse bridles, rusting metal and leather straps, squashed and tattered straw hats, and much, much more, that Faye's befuddled gaze couldn't even begin to take in.

At the end of the hut in the wall was a waist-high aperture with flat slabs of stone laid across inside. It was all cold and dead now, but Faye knew that this was a wood-burning Majorcan oven, and realised with sinking heart that these were all the baking facilities she could expect to find in the farmhouse.

In the corner beside the oven an open fire blazed amidst a hearth of flat stones, and on it a huge iron bowl steamed silently. Faye took a peep into its dark depths. Round mincemeat concoctions in sausage-like skins floated like ghostly apples on the misty water. She backed hastily away and eyed the piles of cooking implements scattered along the other side of the hut.

Like the huge iron bowl on the fire, everything seemed to have been designed for cooking with an army in mind; but after rummaging among the heap, Faye dug out a frying pan slightly less than a cartwheel in size. Discovering the worst as regards kitchen facilities was having no effect on her appetite; whether she liked it or not, she would have to do the best she could with whatever was available.

It seemed, and probably was, hours later when she slumped down at her table in the chimney nook, almost too exhausted to eat.

Things had gone badly from the start. The farmhouse boasted one twentieth-century amenity, a huge fridge, a necessity no doubt in the scorching heat of summer. It was left to Faye to discover where it was hidden away, for during her frantic search Ana was nowhere to be found.

She had unearthed the fridge, festooned with strings of garlic and other pungent-smelling vegetables, behind the door of the room with the walnut furniture, so solving the secret of her missing groceries. Then she had dashed back to the kitchen, only to find Ana poking about as large as life among the pans and looking as though she had been there all day. It had taken some effort on Faye's part to bottle up her irritation now that she had discovered the whereabouts of her provisions.

Both Ana and her husband had obviously received the news of Faye's status in the house from Brent Garrett on his return from the lawyer's office, for Faye had detected a noticeable deference in the couple's manner ever since her own return from Llosaya. Nevertheless, Ana had her husband's supper to prepare, and the long ritual of Majorcan cooking necessitated that she start hours before eating time. To cook her own meal Faye had had to be content with a corner of the fire beside the simmering iron bowl whenever a few red embers became available, which was not very often. The Majorcan woman had gone about her chores in a slow, deliberate way which, coupled with the archaic conditions they were working under, soon had Faye's nerves stretched to snapping point. In preparing her simple meal she could have been finished in half an hour, but as it turned out she was no earlier sitting down to her own supper than the Rodriguez' were in having theirs.

Thankfully now she gulped down the hot sweet tea which had been a work of art to obtain, and munched on a sandwich of crispy bacon, flavoured not unpleasantly with woodsmoke. At least she could count her blessings that there were only two dining tonight at the trestle table behind her, as the farm labourers had gone home earlier. This reduced the cackles and grunts of enjoyment and smacking of greasy lips by half.

Not that Faye had any energy left to let it bother her. She was far too numbed with weariness, brought on by the hectic events of the day, to care a jot one way or the other. Which just went to show, she smiled grimly to herself, how quickly one could get used to a thing when one had to.

The warmth in the inglenook acted like a drug on her senses. A healthy flush on her cheeks after the rawness outdoors, she finished her second cup of tea and lapped up the cosiness like a cat stretching before a blaze. Content after her meal, she could have sat there dozing and dreaming indefinitely, but after a while the fire dropped low, and it began to grow very chilly. Judging by the activity going on behind her Ana and Anofre had finished their supper and were making moves towards going to bed. Work on the farm began at dawn and with an early rise ahead of them it was obvious no more wood would be put on the fire tonight.

Stirring herself, Faye marvelled at the hardy, spartan life the couple led. They had worked all day and expecting no comfort at the end of it, had sat in a draughty room on hard wooden chairs over their evening meal. Now they were going to some icy chamber somewhere beyond the walnut-furnished parlour, blankly unperturbed at what lay ahead of them on the morrow.

For her part Faye would have given anything for an armchair. But as this was never likely to materialise in the farmhouse—she suspected that the couple wouldn't know what to do with one if they saw one— she settled for an early night herself. The idea of curling up luxuriously with a good book or soothing herself with soft music from her transistor radio seemed ludicrous in this draughty barn-like setting.

The cold damp air met her as she entered her room. Ana came behind her and showed her a hook on the wall beside the bed, where she hung the paraffin lamp. Every modern convenience, Faye joked to herself mirthlessly when the woman had gone. Shivering in the pale yellow light, she hurried around turfing out a fleecy nightdress from her cupboard and bedsocks—bedsocks in Majorca! Doggedly she tossed them out. Her feet were already becoming blocks of ice. She was just about to undress when a catastrophic thought hit her. The night clothes she had pulled from the cupboard were still warm and soft after their sojourn by the fire this afternoon. But she had forgotten to do a thing about the bed! What could she do now? Air her sheets? No, the fire was too low. Memories of the Turkish bath ordeal clear in her mind, she pondered furiously and then suddenly dived for her torch. She had an idea!

If anyone had been abroad at that hour they would have wondered what the thin pencil of torchlight was doing wobbling around the courtyard. Faye trod carefully. She expected the confounded dogs to start up their racket at any moment, but true to form in the foul weather, they remained curled up in their shelters.

Inside the cookhouse she rooted around noiselessly, trying to recall where she had seen the old flat-iron earlier. At last her torch beam fell on it among the junk, and she grabbed it and made a hasty retreat back to the house.

When she had raked the dead embers away from the fire in the chimney area, she saw that underneath it still glowed red and fierce. Good! Smiling with satisfaction, she put the flat-iron in among the coals and glided away. Within a few minutes it would be very hot indeed. She would have to be ready.

In her room she hunted around for a thick pad with which to dust off and hold the iron. Then she gave her attention to the bed. After this it was time to hurry back to the fire.

She had only just got back to her room when the door opened.

By now familiar with the primitive plumbing in the house, Faye had elected to stick to washing and cleaning her teeth from the earthenware bowl in her room, which now rested on a wooden chair in the corner. Feeling helpful, Ana had decided to bring her an extra pitcher full of water before turning in for the night herself.

In her ancient, putty-coloured dressing gown tied with string at the waist, her hair flying about in wisps in the draught, the woman's face was a study in dumb astonishment as she stood in the doorway watching Faye painstakingly ironing the bed.

With the top covers folded back, Faye was doing a splendid job of airing the bottom sheet and mattress when she was surprised in the act. She hadn't expected company, but now that she had been caught at it she saw nothing for it but to continue working briskly and nonchalantly as though it was the done thing where she came from to iron one's bed before climbing into it.

Ana's protruding eyes stayed fixed in Faye's direction while she fumbled to put the water down beside the bowl. She came back to the doorway, muttered a strained, '*Buenas noches*,' then dragged her fascinated gaze away from the energetic flurry of the iron and made a hasty departure.

Faye managed to keep going until the door closed, then, lowering the iron, she fell on to the bed and grabbed the sheet to stifle her giggles. She could just imagine the Majorcan's face when she got back to her own room as she told her husband, 'They do some strange things, these English.'

Strange or not, Faye slept slightly better that night, although she suspected that this was due to her colossal fatigue rather than her effort to improve the bed.

The next day she rose determined to view Brent Garrett's section of the *finca*. She had seen all she cared to of the rude construction of the farmhouse.

During the morning she saw Ana going up the outside steps with mop and dusters in her hand. The sleek car was not in the courtyard or in the old lean-to shed which served as a garage. Hitching her washed-out jeans up at the waist and stuffing the bulk of her heavy sweater into them, Faye took another quick look around the courtyard, made sure that Brent Garrett was nowhere about, then casually made for the steps.

Her tour was a disappointing one. In the salon with the dark pictures on the walls where she had been surprised that first night, she passed the open door where Ana was busying herself in the rooms inside, then moved swiftly through into an interior reminiscent of a medieval mansion.

Many of the stone-flagged floors still had carpets, faded and threadbare with time, and rotting tapestries hung on the walls. There were curving flights of stone steps branching off to upper and lower hallways, and high-beamed ceilings which filtered the daylight through dislodged rafters. Several bedrooms boasted porcelain washbasins and most of the other rooms possessed a little furniture which, ugly and old-fashioned as it was, blended in a curious way with the gaunt interiors.

With the smell of dust and decay in her nostrils, Faye made her way back to the outer salon. Ana was still busy in the rooms beyond the open door as she passed; she stopped and peeped inside and then, growing bolder, marched in. After all, she *was* doing a full tour of the *finca*, she told herself. Why shouldn't she see the whole of her inheritance? Somehow she knew that this wasn't the true reason for her impulsive action, but nothing would induce her to admit, not even to herself, that the idea of sneaking a look at her tenant's quarters intrigued her.

As soon as she entered she knew that these were the rooms of the *finca* where the family life must have centred in her grandmother's day and before. There was an all-embracing aura of living here not evident in the rest of the house, as though the walls had soaked up the centuries of animated chatter and laughter; eavesdropped on the sorrows and the tears.

Daylight poured in through the huge windows, their shutters thrown back to light up mellowed floors, solid furniture and faded velvet drapes. The view looked out over the sweep of valley that she had seen yesterday from the grassy terraces. How different it was from the farmhouse where the doorways were the only sources of light; what windows there were being barred and shuttered as though they had never been opened for years. The rooms had recently been made more intimate with additional pieces of furniture, modern and masculine; a high-backed leather armchair beside the open fireplace, a sturdy workbench under the windows in what appeared to serve as a study.

Ana was in the bedroom putting the finishing touches to the bed. Faye called out a greeting as she went by and airily continued on her tour. She noted with envy that there was a bathroom tucked away along a passageway. True, it was fitted out in the ornate, ugly style of the last century, but nevertheless it was a bathroom. Faye eyed it jealously, glowering at the thought of the earthenware bowl and stone pitcher in her room.

At last she made her way back to the main rooms and paused before the work-bench under the windows in the study. This must be where Brent Garrett did most of his work. The books ranged along the back were boringly technical: *The Maintenance and Treatment of Grasses Under Varying Tropical Conditions. Irri-*

gation and Mechanical Field Equipment, and so on. But the watercoloured layouts were fascinating. The man had an eye for detail and colour, she noticed as she studied an attractive map design of the coastal area north of San Mateo. An arrow pointing to a bare expanse inland bore the words along its streamer tail La Zarzamore. *Campo de Golf.*

Engrossed, Faye didn't hear the footsteps from the outer salon and lifted her head only when a voice inside the room said laconically, 'If there's anything you don't understand, just let me know.'

As she spun round she sensed a thread of steel mingling with Brent Garrett's humorous tone. She couldn't blame him for being annoyed at finding her snooping in his private domain; but at the same time she was angry at being caught in the act of looking as though she cared what he did for a living.

He was the first to relax and with his mocking gaze he came to stand beside her at the bench. 'I haven't had time to fill in the details here,' he said drily, indicating the golf layout which she had been so laboriously studying. 'This pink area is where the country club will be. The blue patches are the lakes. Over here you can see....'

Faye swung away, her cheeks burning. 'I'm not in the least bit interested,' she lied. 'I simply came to see if ... well, obviously you're very comfortable here?'

She fought hard to keep the resentment out of her voice. With not much success, it seemed, for Brent Garrett hunched his big shoulders and emphasised with an irritatingly self-satisfied grin, 'Very. If ever you need an extra log for the fire, or somewhere to put your feet up....'

Faye shot him a look of detestation and stalked off, retorting quiveringly, 'There's nothing more insufferable in my opinion than someone who puts on superior airs simply because they've got the best of the bargain.'

Brent Garrett's mocking tones floated after her as she went. 'Feel free to drop in any time.'

For a reply Faye followed Ana out and closed the door forcefully behind her.

That wasn't the last she saw of her tenant that day. In the drizzling outdoors while she endeavoured to keep warm with chores that were necessary anyway, she ran into him several times while crossing the courtyard to and from the cookhouse. She would be struggling with an unwieldy bowl of hot water, or hair hanging over her face, trying to protect a tray of hard-won, congealing food from the icy wind.

He would stroll past to his car to collect items of equipment concerning his job, or to deposit a sheaf of drawing boards in the back. Sometimes he would stop to pass the time of day with Anofre, who might be herding a group of foul-smelling pigs to some new mud heap. If not, there was always Ana serving the dogs with their plates of slop for the day, or scattering corn to the ever-present brood of squawking hens who always got under one's feet.

And when he had finished his conversation with one or the other of them Brent Garrett could always be relied upon to saunter past Faye, oozing superiority and looking unbearably smug as he mounted the steps to his own apartment away from the clatter of the farmyard. Gloweringly she would watch him go as she trudged and worked amidst the squalor. She told herself that if there was any justice in the world it ought to be she who was lording it in the ancestral quarters upstairs, not he!

By the end of the day she was shattered once again from the effort of battling under adverse conditions. She fell into bed in a black mood which was not improved by the persistent dampness of the mattress. She dozed and tossed and turned and fumed. Then finally in the middle of the night she sat bolt upright, rigid with determination. This had gone on long enough. The Spanish overlords of the past might have insisted on keeping their farm subjects in check, but she had no intention of putting up with the out-moded customs of the *finca*. There were rooms upstairs dry and comfortable. Why should she make do with this damp-ridden cell?

She struggled out in the dark and lit the lamp. Then with a cotton negligée covering her nightdress, sheets and blankets tossed over her arm, she went out all set to claim her rights. Brent Garrétt might fancy himself as the despotic type. Well, he would soon learn that she too had an autocratic streak in her!

All was silent in the farmhouse. The stale odour of cooking plus the all-pervading animal smells mingled with the sharp cold air as she crossed the communal kitchen. Outside she was met by the eternal patter of raindrops, and to protect her blankets she crept rapidly up the stone steps.

The great door at the top opened noiselessly at her touch. Her lantern cast an eerie glow in the huge salon. Ignoring the creepy oil paintings with their dozen pairs of dark eyes spying on her movements, she glided swiftly towards the distant entrance.

She already had a bedroom in mind. It was the second door along the first corridor. She remembered it from this morning because it was one of the smallest and therefore decently furnished. Her slippers made no more than a whisper on the stone flags as she went inside. Unwaveringly she tugged the tasselled cord of the bedside lamp, a velvet and parchment affair dusty and yellowed with time, and the light sprang on.

It was an L-shaped room. There were two beds in the wide area and beside them a huge glass window looked out on to a dark well-like enclosure where tubbed trees and shrubbery were open to the rain. In the narrow section of the room a bare wooden table faced another smaller window in the opposite wall, which was shuttered on the inside and wedged across in the small space at the far end was a worn leather settee.

Faye climbed into bed. No cloying dampness here. Admittedly the smell of dust and decay was a little overpowering, but the dryness more than compensated for that. She pulled the sheets around her chin and snuggled down.

She didn't know whether she had dropped off into a doze or not. She supposed it must have been her subconscious playing tricks on her. It was odd how the imagination could distort things when given a free hand. She listened again. It really did sound as though the splattering raindrops had changed direction. Now they weren't raindrops at all, they were a flurry of footsteps and they were outside in the hall. They kept pattering up to her door, stopping, then pattering away again.

Pure imagination, of course, Faye told herself, staunchly closing her ears to the racket. She fell asleep. Half an hour later she awoke feeling an icy cold chill in the room. Her bed was cosy and warm, yet she was seized by an attack of the shivers.

She sat up quickly and switched on the light. The cold air was everywhere in the room. And that wasn't all. With a creepy feeling she looked down at herself. The hairs on her forearms were standing rigid, each on a separate goose-pimple.

She turned to look out of the window, and saw the greenery and leaf fronds battering and rustling against the glass. A spine-tingling thought struck her. Supposing some of her grandmother's ancestors had been laid to rest out there beneath the stone flags and those potted shrubs!

She told herself the idea was absurd. Slowly she trained her gaze around the room. In the yellowish light everything was just the same; the bare wooden table against the wall in the narrow section at the foot of the beds, the dusty settee wedged in the space at the far end.

Reassured, Faye switched off the light again and dropped back among the pillows. But her heart was thudding madly as she tried to get back to sleep. Though she told herself she was getting nervy for no reason, her insides tightened up at every sound.

And then she heard it—a long, heartfelt shuddering sigh from down by the settee.

She leapt up, terror paralysing her efforts to find the light cord. The room sprang to life. It was exactly as it had been a few minutes before.

Faye stared hard towards the settee. That too was unchanged, like the rest of the room notable only for its bareness. Grimly she donned her cotton negligée and slipped into her mules. If there *was* something there ... invisible or not .... Bracing herself, she walked towards the settee.

She was almost there when the inside shutter on the window opposite the table swung open with a slow, grinding creak.

That was all Faye needed. There was no reason for the shutter to swing open. There were no draughts, nothing. It was simply a window adjoining another room. Her nerves, keyed up to panic pitch, snapped completely at the agonised sound of the squealing hinges. She stared at the slowly moving shutter, let out a piercing scream and ran for her life.

Out of the room, along the corridor, stumbling, fumbling, whirling round, she fled as though every conceivable horror was hot on her tail. It was dark, and that made matters worse; instinct alone guided her towards the main salon. Fleeing wildly, a wraith-like vision in the shadows, she crossed its huge echoing spaces and ran straight into the arms of Brent Garrett.

CHAPTER FOUR

As soon as Faye made contact with the dressing-gowned figure, all her fears left her. A horrible foolish feeling flooded in now as she clung to the hard masculine form.

Brent Garrett's tones, though laced with irritability, were also vibrantly mocking as he held her close and drawled, 'Do you *always* make a habit of floating around in the middle of the night?'

Aware of her arms still clasped tightly around his neck, Faye pushed away from him and gabbled, still breathless, 'I thought I'd try sleeping up here ...' she pointed a shaking finger towards the alcove entrance, 'but the rooms ... they're spooky....'

'Have you only just noticed?' her lodger replied in maddeningly cheerful tones.

Faye glowered at him. 'I suppose you think it's funny,' she snapped. 'Well, as far as I'm concerned you're welcome to your manorial *friends*!'

As she marched towards the outside door Brent Garrett called after her banteringly, 'Goodnight, Miss Chalmers. Sleep well.'

She retorted with an icy smile, 'Goodnight, Mr Garrett. Don't worry, I will.'

In her flimsy night attire she froze on the journey down the outside steps and along to her room in the farmhouse. Fumbling crossly in the darkness, she dressed in slacks and woollies and slept under a pile of coats.

Faye did no more internal exploring after that. She drove down to Llosaya and bought two hot water bottles for her bed and with the sticks of furniture which Ana produced from time to time she was able to make her room passably comfortable.

The weather now was her chief frustration. Where was the sunny Majorca she had known in the past? Why had no one told her about the rain? It came down day after day and ran in rivulets away from the house, drenching the countryside until it was truly water-logged.

Occasionally the sky would lighten, giving one false hope for a while, then back would come the dark clouds with a renewed downpour. Faye used these brief intervals of calm to investigate the outside of the *finca*. Swathed in heavy sweaters to combat the freezing wind, she walked to get the exercise; it would have been useless to fool herself into believing that she derived any other benefit from viewing her dismal surroundings.

San Mateo, she discovered, was built on a hillside. Its rear section looked out over flat land towards the main road to Llosaya, its south walls faced out over the wide valley and looked across to a line of pine-clad hills. The mountains, invariably hidden in the mist these days, towered away to the west beyond the end of the valley.

The lane that led in from the main road curved round a cement hummock on which the cookhouse and other nondescript buildings stood, and then swerved down into the valley. Occasionally a car took the peril-ous route down, for it was recognised as a public right of way, linking up with another main road across the valley. A steep hillside path directly alongside the *finca* and flanked by a line of stately trees could only be negotiated on foot.

During her brief excursions out of doors Faye had plenty of time to view the dogs tethered in various spots around the cement stretch of courtyard. Now when she passed, no longer hostile, they would show themselves writhing shyly close to the ground and whining for affection.

All the dogs, true to the Spaniards' love of the dramatic, answered to names which bordered on the romantic: *Tarzan, Falcon, Perlita.* . . . Faye wished that their conditions befitted their grand titles, but she knew better than to try to change things too rapidly around the farmhouse. That would be the surest way to make herself unpopular. Slowly, carefully over the weeks she would contrive to introduce a straw mat or two into their bleak cement shelters. And a little at a time she could lengthen the dogs' tethers. That way no one would be offended.

The Rodriguez couple were taking to the idea of having her as a permanent resident in the farmhouse. Ana, in her slow dour way, was eager to introduce her to the mysteries of Majorcan cooking. Anofre, Faye suspected, had sneakingly accepted her from the start. His faded brown eyes alight with mischief, he derived great satisfaction from showing her all the chores he had to attend to around the farmhouse. And there was his work in the fields.

One morning he went to great lengths to show her, as they stood on the crown of the hill in the courtyard, the area that he farmed. The rows of grapevines, a great patch of land below in the valley, belonged to the *finca*, he told her; as did the rolling stretches adjoining, planted with broad beans, maize, sweet grass and fig trees.

And the expanse to the west, he continued. Over there where a circular copse was a dot on the corn-fields and the almond groves stretched away clear up to the foot of the pine-clad slopes. And the fields where the sheep grazed beyond the ribbon of road in the distance. All this and much more of the flat land behind the house belonged to San Mateo.

Faye felt truly a queen surveying her property. To

think that all this was part of her inheritance. The only thing that irked her during these glowing moments was Brent Garrett's mocking presence nearby. He had come down to collect a batch of fresh towels from Ana and lingered while she went off to dust around his rooms, he smoking a cigarette.

Faye had a feeling that he knew all there was to know about the contents of her grandmother's will. It hadn't taken her long to gather that he and Don José Andrés were good friends, and no doubt they would have talked together about her position at the *finca*. She could feel his quizzical glance on her now as she sparkled over the view. Perhaps the conditions of her inheritance amused him? The fact that one day she would have to find a Spanish husband, if the wealth of San Mateo was truly to be hers?

Brent Garrett, like Faye, was confined to the *finca* because of the interminable rain, but of course he had his designing work to keep him occupied in his rooms. Faye longed to get outdoors and paint. Since this was going to be her only source of income, every day's lost earnings were a minor catastrophe when she thought of her precarious financial position.

But she couldn't get out. If it wasn't raining it was freezing cold, and to have to set up an easel in the piercing north wind would have been asking for pneumonia. Instead she wrote a glowing letter home about how wonderful she was finding everything at the *finca*, and amused herself making indoor sketches of the farmhouse.

After two weeks, however, she was bored to distraction. It was one afternoon when she was turning out her handbag that she came across a card on which was printed the words *Hotel Azalea, Porto Cristo*. Of course! The Templetons! She could pay them a visit. They had told her to drop in any time, and she badly

61

needed someone to pour out her troubles to.

So, dressed for the outdoors, she turned her back on the ugly old *finca* with its gaping hole above the court-yard; on the farmyard clutter and smells, on the annoying thought of her tenant living in blissful seclusion upstairs, and climbed into her little car and drove off.

The occasional lull in the rain had allowed the stretches of water to subside a little, nevertheless Faye found it a tiresome business steering along the country roads eastwards. When she emerged on to the main highway out to the coast conditions improved.

She found Porto Cristo in a winding bay. It was probably a pretty little spot in the summer, but now its red roofs and white tower were misted over with drizzle and looked drab under the sullen grey skies.

The Hotel Azalea was not difficult to locate. A tall narrow building, painted white, it stood out above the tumbling rocks and pine clumps around the curve of the tiny bay. Faye drove up the steep incline curving round alongside the beach and into a long narrow *calle* behind the cliffside establishments. Then, parking her car, she approached the rear entrance of the Hotel Azalea.

There was much activity inside the gates. Workmen were painting the metal legs of tables and chairs in a sheltered area on the tiny terrace and a couple of plump women argued volubly in Mallorquene over the arranging of flower pots along the low walls. Bart Templeton, spruce as ever, his navy blue sweater and slacks expensively casual, was up a pair of steps outside the dining room window fiddling delicately with a jammed sun-canopy. Through the open window beside him Greta, sparkling and colourful in an emerald green suit and beige blouse, let out a yelp of delight. 'It's Faye!'

Bart wobbled on the steps as she began to climb

frantically out of the window. He said with his usual goodnatured grin, 'Steady on, old girl, or she'll be scraping us both up from the terrace.'

Greta disentangled herself from the step-ladder and embraced Faye warmly. Her sky-blue eyes were wide and probing as she looked up at her. 'What happened? We'd given you up.'

'It took me a little time to get myself sorted out,' Faye smiled. Overcome with a sudden bout of shyness, she glanced up at the troublesome sun canopy and queried lightly, 'Having trouble?'

Greta tilted an eyebrow. 'Oh, it works perfectly if we unroll it *inside* and suffocate the guests with it while they're dining.' She was struck by a sudden thought and called brightly aloft, 'Hey! Why don't we just turn the roll around?'

'No go.' Her husband shook his head over the metal roller socket. 'The damned thing's jammed tighter than a rivet in the Eiffel Tower.' He tossed his screwdriver down in disgust and winked at Faye. 'Anyway, I think it's a good excuse to stop and have a cup of tea.'

'What a marvellous idea!' Greta tucked her arm in Faye's and led her towards the door. 'The boss says we can take a break.'

They relaxed in chintzy armchairs in a small lounge overlooking the beach. Most of the furniture in the hotel was covered with dust-sheets, but this was obviously a room in the Templetons' private quarters. Bart left the girls to enjoy a female get-together and went off in his carefree way to organise the tea.

Greta wriggled in her chair, eager to hear all the news. As soon as they were alone she asked brightly, 'Well, how are you settling in?'

Faye pulled a face. She said drily, 'Not too bad. The *finca* turned out to be a centuries-old ruin, but I get on well with the farm animals. We're practically roommates.'

'Oh no!' Greta's face was filled with concern. 'That's what we tried to tell you on the boat, darling. So many people come to the island believing they've found El Dorado or Nirvana or whatever it is.' She looked penitently at Faye. 'You were so starry-eyed and optimistic on that first night we didn't have the heart to disillusion you.'

'It's maybe as well you didn't,' Faye said wryly. 'Had I known what I was in for I would probably have turned tail and gone haring back home.'

Greta nodded soberly. Then she snatched up the subject again and hurried on enquiringly, 'But surely there's somewhere decent to live in this ... inheritance of yours?'

'Oh, there are plenty of rooms in the *finca*!' Faye gave an ironic little smile. 'The only trouble is, the ghosts of the last two or three hundred years appear to have a firm hold on the place and seem determined to keep it that way.'

'No! Really?' Greta looked hugely amused, and more so when Faye gave her a potted version of her recent experience when trying to sleep there.

'Not only that,' Faye continued to unload her cares, 'I arrived to find that the only habitable section of the *finca* had been let without my knowledge.'

Greta's laughing blue eyes almost leaped out of their sockets. 'Darling, you *haven't* got a *lodger*?'

'Unfortunately, yes,' Faye nodded grimly. 'It wasn't my doing. He was there when I arrived. He and the family lawyer-cum-estate-agent have got it all nicely cooked between them. The result is that I'm stuck with him for a year.'

'Ooh, how awful!' Greta giggled, trying to maintain a shocked look. 'What's he like?'

'Oh ... thirtyish....' *Aggravatingly sure of himself*, Faye wanted to say, but refrained. 'Medium height ...

brown hair ... you know the type.'

'Yes, I know the type....' Greta nodded vaguely.

'He's English,' Faye added as an afterthought, 'and he's designing a golf course, of all things, somewhere outside Caliséta.'

'A golf course? *Designing a golf course?*' Greta shot to the edge of her chair. 'Hey, he doesn't happen to have a lusciously muscular physique, does he? and hair that crinkles ... and a kind of slow infectious grin?'

'You could describe him like that, I suppose,' Faye admitted sourly.

Greta gabbled on, 'It wouldn't be a man called Brent, would it ... Brent Garrett?'

'I believe that is his name,' Faye replied coldly.

With a squeal of delight Greta leapt up from her chair and almost collided with her husband, who was bringing in the tea tray. 'Guess who's over at Caliséta?' she cried amid the clatter, 'Brent Garrett!'

Bart steadied the wobbling crockery, patient as ever, and popped the scattered sugar lumps back in the bowl. 'Well, the old son of a gun! What's he doing over there?'

'Designing a golf course, what else!'

'I take it you know this Brent Garrett?' Faye asked, trying to cover her frozen smile with a film of warmth.

'Know him!' Bart grinned, putting the tray down carefully on the coffee table in front of them. 'He's one of my old buddies.'

'Men are always so possessive,' his wife scolded him sweetly, and turned to Faye. 'Actually we got to know Brent when we were launching a small hotel on the Costa del Sol. He was the golf architect for the La Zafar course down there. You should see it now ... palm trees, lakes, a fabulous country club,' Greta lapsed lyrical.

'I think I have heard of it,' Faye admitted stiltedly.

'It's where all the big championships are played,' Greta fell back in her chair and hugged herself reminiscently. 'Oh, those were the days! We had fun by the barrow-load, didn't we, Bart?'

Her husband nodded. 'We'll have to run over and pay old Brent a visit some time.'

He turned to draw up a chair and feeling that some comment was expected of her Faye said stiffly, 'I'm sure he'll be glad to know he's got friends on the island.'

Settling himself, Bart chuckled, 'If I know Brent, he'll have made a few already. He never was one to stick fast for company.'

Greta woke up to the fact that tea had to be poured. Sitting beside Faye, she eyed the piles of cakes and biscuits and scoffed with amusement, 'Can't you tell when the men are let loose in the kitchen? They think that every cup of tea is an excuse for an eating orgy.'

'Well, why not?' Bart rubbed his hands over the tray. 'I for one could polish off this lot without any bother.'

Glad that the subject of Brent Garrett had been dropped, Faye joined in the frivolities. After her second cup of tea, she said, 'The biggest shock to me is the weather. I never knew it could rain like this in Majorca.'

'Lots of people don't,' Greta responded. 'They come here in the summer and think we bask in the heat all the year round. Bart and I have been here three years, and we've seen snow on the mountains in May and wind that can freeze you while you're standing.'

'I've sampled it already, thank you,' Faye said, shivering at the thought.

'Comes from the Pyrenees,' Bart said knowingly. 'Wait until you see some of our thunderstorms. They're like something straight out of Dante's Inferno.'

'That's right, cheer the girl up!' Greta drained the teapot and they all laughed at the gloomy topic they had chosen.

'What gets me,' Faye said, a flush on her cheeks after the hot tea, 'is that nobody appears to mind the rain. The islanders seem to think it's one huge joke.'

'Which to them it is,' Bart pointed out. 'There may seem a lot of it about to you, but you've got to remember we've had a drought for eight months. Without this break in the weather there was a high risk of crop failure. Naturally they're happy,' he grinned, lowering his empty plate. 'The Majorcans hide from the sun and they hate the wind, but they love the rain. To them it means money.'

The sky was darkening towards evening when Faye said goodbye to the Templetons. Disregarding the rain-drops, they walked with her to the gate and watched her climb into her car. As she was starting up Greta waved and called, 'Give our love to Brent.'

Faye's features froze. 'I don't see all that much of him.'

Between themselves the Templetons exchanged glances, pretending not to notice her shut-down expression. As she passed the gate they called in unison, 'Drive carefully!'

' 'Bye,' Faye smiled, and waved and drove off. On the way back to the *finca* she couldn't help feeling disappointed with the afternoon as a whole. She liked the Templetons more each time she saw them and she had thoroughly enjoyed their company; but the whole purpose of her visit had been to find a nice comfortable shoulder to cry on. She had come to relate the full woeful story of what she was having to put up with at San Mateo, expecting the sympathy to flow like balm over her wounds. It had been a bit of a blow to discover that the Templetons and Brent Garrett were old friends.

Curse the man! She swished her way gloweringly along the country roads. There seemed to be no way past that self-assured conceit of his. It appeared that *he* was friends with everyone around here, whereas *she* didn't have one ally!

February came, bringing the sunshine and buffeting breezes. Stallions of white clouds galloped across the blue expanse of sky chasing away the grey wisps of winter. The mountains touched with rays of pearly-pink light rose like fairytale castles out of the valley mists. Just to be outdoors on these days filled one with a sense of drama.

Faye walked, startled to find the almond trees already heavy with blossom. It was almost as though the change had taken place overnight. Farm-workers were trimming the grapevines. Sheep grazed, the bells they wore clanging musically. The line of aspen trees bordering the meadow at the foot of the hill was dusted with spring green. The scene filled Faye with a new surge of vigour, a fresh sense of purpose. The sun was warm. Now was the time to paint. But she hadn't reckoned for the tantalizing breezes.

It had long been her desire to paint the colourful cockerel who strutted around the courtyard. He was no friend of hers, for it was he who tugged her out of her dreams at first light each morning with his lusty, alarm-clock crowing. However, he was a fascinating subject with his ruby-brown feathers touched with rust, crimson and orange and even a dash of turquoise; and his splendid glistening black spray of a tail. Faye was longing to put him on canvas.

On a sparkling morning, a tune on her lips at being able to get outdoors at last, she fastened a blue linen paint-smock over her dress, and with a matching wide headband to keep her hair from her face as she went to work.

The cockerel's favourite haunt was on a mound of old animal fodder dumped opposite the low out-buildings at the edge of the courtyard. Spotting him there, as he pecked abstractedly in between preening his magnificent plumage, Faye carted over her painting materials which took two or three journeys.

The wind had merely seemed playful on these trips. It was when she had settled down to do a quick sketch that she realised what mischief it could get up to. First it tossed her paintbrushes and crayons down into the dust, then it opened the pages of her drawing pad and flapped distractingly through them, leaving them limp and dog-eared. Determined to be the master, Faye fetched rocks and stones to act as paperweights. She had just got everything anchored down and was about to start some serious work when a particularly heavy gust whipped the canvas from her easel and set it down with a clatter which made the cockerel scuttle up to the top of the heap in a nervous flurry of feathers and wings.

Well, there was a remedy for everything, Faye told herself cheerfully, going indoors for a ball of string. She had what she considered the brilliant idea of tying the canvas to the easel, and securing the rear legs of the easel to a nearby post. But when she tried to put this idea into practice the wind proved to be cleverer than she was. It flapped, tugged and meddled delight-edly around the canvas so that Faye needed half a dozen pairs of hands just to hold it down, let alone secure it. But hold it down she would!

All her smiling good humour evaporated in the struggle. The tug-of-war became an out-and-out battle between her and the wind. She considered she had a personal score to settle with it by this time, and beat it she would, if it was the last thing she did.

Of course Brent Garrett would have to choose that particular moment to drive in from the lane!

Faye didn't notice the car. She was busy trying to extricate her wrists and ankles from the mess of string while gripping the canvas which was waving about like a yacht sail in the breeze, when his tones, laced with irony, drifted over. 'Having trouble?'

Faye turned sharply and saw him sitting there watching lazily from his car window a few feet away. She smiled frigidly. 'Nothing that I can't cope with, thank you.'

Making no move to go, he surveyed the situation leisurely. 'The wind's coming over the brow of the hill. If you move in closer to the house, you'll miss most of it.'

Faye gave him a scathing look and replied sweetly, jerking a thumb at the cockerel, 'My subject here prefers his heap to the courtyard. Any ideas on how I can paint him without using a telescope?'

Brent Garrett shrugged and said casually, 'If it was me I'd throw a few grains of corn into one of those hen coops.' He nodded to the pile beside her. 'Slip the catch when he's in, and you've got him on ice for as long as you want.'

Faye was rendered speechless at the simplicity of the idea, which did nothing to improve her temper. There was nothing more infuriating, when battling with a problem, than someone who offered brilliant suggestions which you hadn't thought of yourself. Especially when that someone was Brent Garrett.

She went on struggling with the flapping canvas which fancied itself as a kite and couldn't wait to take off, and replied with a perverse smile, 'Thank you for the advice, but I prefer to do it my way, if you don't mind.'

Brent Garrett gave her his know-it-all gleam and turned away to park his car. 'Just trying to help.'

In time Faye learned to beat the wind which gathered strength in the evenings, blowing precious

70

almond trees and huge carobs across the roads, and shattering flower-pots and roof-tiles in the villages. Ana told her it was the Xalloc, which came straight across the plain at this time of the year. Faye lay terrified in her bed at nights as it roared, thundered and pounded on the walls. Now she knew why the *finca's* broad back and windowless walls faced out on to the open plain, and its tiled roof sloped down towards its courtyard and terraces huddled in shelter above the valley. Ugly it might be, but as a monstrous slab of stone nothing could shake it; the fact that it had stood up to centuries of spring batterings by the Xalloc said something for its construction.

Happily these wind storms were short-lived, and in the mornings with the brilliant sunshine and vivid blue skies one could almost forget they had happened. Faye didn't complain then about the playful breezes. But though she learned to avoid them by choosing her work spots carefully, nowhere was safe, she discovered, from the laconic humour of her tenant.

Returning from his work out of doors, he would come up behind her when she was intent on putting some scene on canvas, and make her almost start off the stool at the sound of his lazy voice in her ear. He fancied himself as a critic, much to her annoyance. And she was ruffled for another reason; most of the time when he passed judgement on her efforts, she knew he was right.

Once, when she was trying to capture the two big bluffs in the mountains from one of the grassy terraces, he strolled in through the gateway from the courtyard and said breezily over her shoulder, 'Your perspective's all wrong. You need a tree or something in the foreground, and the bluffs would look better with a touch of ultramarine. But don't worry,' he lifted a hand in mock protest as she threatened to throw the paint palette at him, 'you'll get it.'

'I will.' She gave him a thin smile. 'Without the help of someone who has nothing to do but paint pretty pictures of golf courses all day.'

He thrust his hands into his pockets, annoyingly oblivious to her acid mood, and grinned, 'There's a little more to my work than that. If you want to know what really goes on in the laying out and building of an eighteen-hole golf course, drop in at La Zarzamora and see for yourself. I'll be happy to show you around.'

'No, thanks,' Faye stabbed at the canvas with her brush and shot him a vitriolic glance. 'I see enough of you around the house.'

Brent Garrett gave her his obnoxiously self-satisfied grin, and murmured as he moved off, 'That's me! Always a hit with my flatmates.'

Though Faye told herself she hated these joking interruptions, when her tenant took to spending more and more time away from the *finca*, she found she missed his bantering comments. Not for the world would she admit this, of course. She was turning out a picture every four or five days now. And that, she told herself, was her only concern at the moment, to build up a stock of paintings ready for the approaching tourist season.

Nevertheless, there were days when the sun shone warmly and the countryside, heavy with the perfume and promise of spring, was almost too much to take in its beauty, so that Faye would feel a powerful upsurge of yearning for she knew not what.

On these days the sight of her oil paints and easel depressed her. One afternoon, shirking the idea of work, she backed out her little blue car into the court-yard and drove off. She knew roughly where the new golf course was situated, so why not take a run out there? Purely for something to do, of course, she convinced herself, and casually swung the wheel in that direction.

Already she was feeling better for taking the break. The air was sparklingly clear, the view of rolling green fields and blossoming stretches inspiring to the eye. La Zarzamora was only a few miles from the *finca*. In a short time Faye was looking out over a barren area which continued clear up to a line of granite slopes in the distance. The ground was being churned up by all kinds of grotesque machines, and muddy puddles dotted the landscape.

Unimpressed, Faye followed the temporary road which snaked around mountains of earth and piles of rocks. She passed an occasional wooden hut, but saw no signs of life. She was beginning to think there was no one about apart from the men in the machines, when a turn in the road brought her to a cluster of temporary buildings, and here luxury cars were parked. Though the surrounding red earth was ridged and ugly and all kinds of implements littered the area, the atmosphere around the main hut was that of an already thriving country club.

Near the sleek and opulent cars Faye spotted Brent Garrett. He was wearing coffee-coloured overalls and an orange-coloured safety helmet, both of which accentuated his tan in a devastating way. Not that she would let herself dwell on that, for she was too intent on boring a hole through the cluster of feminine forms which almost blocked him from view.

Without knowing it, her lips became a set line as she advanced. Her eyes never left the waving, silken dark tresses and elegant trouser-clad behinds. She had heard of the saying *a bevy of beautiful girls*, but this was ridiculous! Dark-eyed and long-limbed, they hung about the cars like a spray of exotic flowers. Listening to the laughter, Faye had half a mind to turn round and go back to her own car, but some grim sense of purpose made her press on.

Brent Garrett was the first to get wind of her approach, his blue glance swerved in on her, he stirred himself and drawled mockingly, 'Well, look who's come to pay us a visit. The oil queen herself!'

A slim reed-like creature in leaf-green slacks and waistcoat widened her gaze. 'You mean she's an oil heiress?'

'No, I mean she paints with it,' Brent Garrett quipped, leaving the beauty with a blank look.

Faye eyed him tartly. In her old jeans and faded sweater she had to suffer the curious, slightly hostile glances of the polished butterflies as she observed, 'I see I'm not the only one who gets the offer of a conducted tour around the place!'

'They're from the villa,' Brent Garrett grinned, jerking a thumb towards a white house in the distance. He didn't have the decency to look sheepish.

Faye said woodenly, 'Well, as you're so occupied I won't stay to take up more of your time.'

'It's okay,' Brent Garrett grabbed her arm easily, 'the girls are just going.' He made a shooing gesture, and to the cries of disappointment from the fluttering femininity he replied soothingly, ushering them on their way, 'We'll be over later for a drink. *Hasta luego.*'

Faye watched the long gleaming cars disappear one by one across the muddy stretches. She couldn't take her eyes off the rambling villa in the distance; it was the only house to be seen in this wild expanse of open country.

Brent Garrett drawled in her ear, 'Shall we go?'

Faye dragged her glance away and turned. She couldn't think what they were going to look at in these barren, churned up surroundings, but surprisingly enough she found the tour interesting.

She was guided across the ridges of earth to a mechanical monster, which proved to be able to amble along in a leisurely manner despite its ungainly appearance. Strapped in her seat alongside Brent Garrett at the wheel, she felt a tiny thrill of excitement.

She sneaked a glance at him now and again as they rocked and lurched over the uneven ground. She supposed he must be somewhere in his early thirties. She watched his strong brown hands working the levers, and thought how different he looked like this from the man she had come upon that first night at the *finca*. He had been wearing an elegant smoking jacket then, and had had all the airs of the proverbial Lord of the Manor.

And she mustn't forget, she told herself firmly, that this was the role he was determined to play at San Mateo. When he turned to slant her his mocking gleam, although her heart fluttered idiotically at the sight of his smile and his strong white teeth, her head demanded that she kept her gaze directed coolly towards the outdoors.

They had an uncluttered view from the elevated cabin. 'We've had to bulldoze more than a million cubic metres of earth,' she was informed lazily as they travelled over the rough ground. 'There were several small hills which would have interfered with fairway planning. The land has been surveyed for prevailing winds and over there,' Brent pointed to the outer perimeter facing seawards where men were working beside loaded lorries, 'we're planting banks of trees to break the wind pattern. Later we'll plan the natural hazards, tree clumps and rough.'

Faye never knew that so much went into the planning of a golf course. As they encircled the area she learned all about the checking for direction of flight of golf balls so as not to hazard the public, the weeding, sewing, ploughing and levelling of the land and preparing turfs for greens and tees.

When they arrived back at the group of huts, Brent told her, 'This is the site for the clubhouse. We can

75

take a look at the designs in my office if you're interested.'

But Faye's curiosity remained with the white villa in the distance. She said offhandedly, 'Didn't you say we were going over to the house for a drink?'

'Sure thing, if that's what you want,' Brent swung the levers, and they went ambling over the ground like some giant, unwieldy beetle.

As they approached Faye saw that the mountains served as an impressive backcloth for the villa. It was much bigger than she had imagined and seemed to be set inside its own walled grounds. It had an ornate porticoed entrance, outside which Brent brought the machine to a stop. He helped Faye down, then led her inside with a casual, self-possessed air which irritated her.

Brent's hand on her arm, Faye was guided through a dim tastefully furnished interior: he seemed to know his way around all right, she thought sourly. They emerged and followed leafy paths to where a sparkling swimming pool was the dominant feature of a secluded area in the grounds.

It was too cold for swimming, but the March sunshine trapped between high walls and luxurious growth allowed for light garments. These were disported to the best possible advantage by the slender occupiers of the lounging chairs and garden divans at the pool-side.

In her old farm clothes Faye felt like a fish out of water among the Spanish beauties. In her opinion the women of Spain, with their liquid black eyes and lustrous dark hair, were among the most attractive in the world, but she didn't find this a very cheering thought just now.

She was introduced to all of them, and had her hand clasped limply here and there before being offered a chair. There was no more warmth here, she noticed,

76

than there had been on her first encounter with the girls beside the workmen's huts.

A maid in a black dress served drinks while the girls talked in voluble Spanish. Faye gave no indication that she knew the language, leaving all the conversation to Brent. This seemed to suit the cluster of females perfectly. She doubted whether she would have got a word in anyway; they were more than happy to monopolise Brent's attention.

As though he sensed a cold front between his hostesses and Faye, he drained his glass and said cheerfully, 'Well, I've got to be getting back to work.'

The girls gave their usual wails of lament at the parting. As for Faye, she got up and strolled towards the leafy opening and no one even noticed. When Brent joined her she gave a polite wave and withdrew.

She made the trip out to the mechanical conveyance coolly, with a bright couldn't care-less attitude. When they were seated in the elevated cabin and doing their spider-crawl back towards the huts Brent explained with a lazy grin, though Faye did her best to look indifferent:

'The villa belongs to a Barcelona business family. The girls come over from time to time for a change of scene.' He swung the levers as they crawled up and over a mound of rocks. 'Daughters, nieces and so forth of upper-class Spanish families do very little work.'

'So I've noticed,' Faye replied caustically.

'The girls are taken up with the idea of learing English,' Brent said with his blue gleam, 'hence my popularity.'

'Oh, I'm sure it's something more than that!' Faye gave him a condescending smile.

Ignoring her barbed tones, he went on placidly, 'They like to speak it when they come out to the site.'

Recalling the passable accent of the sylph-like girl in the leaf-green outfit, Faye retorted, 'There didn't seem to be much wrong with the bit I heard.'

Brent shrugged easily, and glancing her way replied with his aggravatingly smooth grin, 'Practice makes perfect.'

Back at the huts Faye allowed him to help her down from her seat, huffily. Flicking a look back in the direction they had come, she said tartly, 'It's a beautiful villa with every modern comfort. I wonder you didn't choose to make your base there instead of San Mateo.'

Brent's hands hadn't left her waist, and with his blue gaze close to hers he drawled, 'If I lived at the villa I wouldn't get much work done.'

Faye felt herself blushing and swinging away, she marched, half stumbling, back to her car. It jerked forward over the uneven ground, and tore off along the dirt road.

He was really the most infuriating man she had ever met!

CHAPTER FIVE

As far as living at the *finca* was concerned, Faye was convinced that fate could hold no more surprises. She was wrong. But for once, she found the unexpected rather pleasant.

It was an afternoon when she had just settled down to work at her easel. She had chosen her subject some days before, the rolling fields and low windmill-topped hills, a view one received when looking immediately across from the farmhouse doorway. The windmills had long since lost their sails, and try as she might Faye couldn't capture the faded rose colour of the stonework—much less their antiquated look.

The spring sunshine was warm on her shoulders as

she sat perched on the brow of the courtyard slope. When she heard the soft footfall behind her she thought it was Brent come to tease her, until a voice gushed in deep musical Spanish, 'The windmills are perfect! And I like the sky and the pretty white clouds.'

Faye turned and rose hurriedly. The man negotiating the last few steps of the cart track up from the valley protested, 'Oh, please don't get up!' then grabbed her hand and kissed it. 'El Conde de Canyaret. Enrique Castaño at your service.' Then, as Faye could do nothing but stand completely mesmerised by his smile, 'We're neighbours, you know.' He pointed across the valley to a distant blur of stonework among the pine trees. 'I considered it was high time that I came and made your acquaintance, and of course,' he gazed into her eyes lingeringly, 'welcomed you to our country.'

'I'm very happy to know you,' Faye said, to give her time to take in this human whirlwind.

He was tall with an arrogant swagger, but apart from this there was little to indicate his Spanish nobility, for his dark grey suit was crumpled and shiny with wear. His hair, greying at the temples, was shaggily long, as was the moustache following the wide curving line of his upper lip. Without all the facial hair Faye reckoned he couldn't be much older than Brent.

She barely had time to recover her equilibrium when another figure appeared round the bend of the cart track. It was that of a Spanish woman, round of figure and buxomly made, puffing and panting as she covered the last few yards up the hill. She made no effort to hide her annoyance at being left behind.

Much to Faye's surprise, the Conde took her arm and turned away as though he had noticed nothing. She looked back, feeling obliged to offer a polite smile of welcome to this second visitor, and when he saw that there was no way of avoiding the introduction the Conde sighed.

'Oh, this is ... an old friend of mine, Señorita Carmina del Flores.'

Faye's smile turned to one of apology and she waved an arm towards the farmhouse. 'I'm afraid I can't offer you much in the way of comfort, but you're very welcome all the same.'

Despite her late arrival, Carmina Flores appeared to wield an iron control. It was she who said, with a rapier-like glance at the Conde, 'Please don't worry. We are only staying a moment.'

Attractive in a smouldering, sultry way, with her oiled black hair drawn into a gleaming bun at the back of her proud head and her heavily made-up black eyes ablaze with her forceful personality, she led the way into the courtyard. In her red spotted dress, frilled at the neckline and the lower hem, she looked as though she moved in a flamenco rhythm.

Ana was carrying a bowl of slops out to the pig troughs, but set it down when she saw the company, greeting Carmina Flores with a noticeable deference in her manner. The Conde might just as well not have existed for all the notice she took of him. Though he showed not the slightest discomfort Faye was conscious of the rebuff, and said hurriedly, 'I don't think I've introduced myself. I'm——'

'Señorita Chalmers ... Faye Chalmers. Is that not so?' The Conde seized the opportunity to take her hand in his and kiss it once again.

'How did you know?' Faye laughed her surprise.

'Oh, word gets around.' The Conde smiled, pinning her like a startled butterfly with his gaze. It was dark and intense, but it was also full of fun, and one black eyebrow quirked in a saucy way when he talked.

Ana and Carmina Flores, their discordant Spanish voices raised as though the farm was under siege, were politely engaged in domestic chat. The Conde, still holding Faye's hand, urged, with a sly glance over his shoulder, 'Shall we walk?'

Faye had the feeling that he found the Spanish woman's company rather tiresome. Before she knew where she was they were rounding the farm buildings on the edge of the lane, and although she had only just met the Conde she couldn't deny a secret thrill at being swept away like this. Once they were out of sight of the others he spoke playfully, but on the alert, as though he expected to be interrupted at any moment. 'In a way you and I are related, you know.'

'I don't believe it!' Faye gasped laughingly.

'It's true,' he insisted with that heart-twanging smile of his, 'I'm the only remaining relative of that dear departed old lady Doña Maria Lopez de Chalmers.'

'My grandmother!' Faye stared in wonder.

'But for you I would have inherited San Mateo.' The Conde's injured look was tempered by humour. 'However, I don't intend to be churlish about this. I'm sure you and I are going to be great friends.'

The voices in the courtyard stopped and like a prisoner knowing that his time is up the Conde hurriedly raised her hand. She felt the warmth of his lips as he brushed them lingeringly over her skin and with her gaze drowning in his, he murmured, 'We mustn't let it be too long before we see each other again.'

Faye's legs grew weak. She was being transported dreamily into a world of strumming harp strings and a choir of angels' voices when the strident blare of a car horn shattered the spell. She turned to see the bonnet of Brent's car brushing her skirts.

The Conde disappeared at the sharp call of 'Enrique!' from the courtyard, and by the time Faye had recovered herself sufficiently to follow he and Carmina Flores were fading from view down the cart track leading into the valley.

Nudging his way testily into the courtyard, Brent said with an odd twist to his smile, 'Who's the character with the smoochy charm?'

'Oh, just a visitor of mine,' Faye returned airily. Her eyes were shining from the encounter, but more than this it gave her a peculiar feeling of elation to know that Brent was ruffled by what he had seen.

'Well, you might tell him the lane entrance is hardly the place to do his Don Juan stuff.' Brent slammed the door of his car rather forcefully.

'I shall entertain my guests wherever it suits me,' Faye retorted loftily, 'and anyone with manners would have been perfecty happy to wait.'

'I've got a golf course to finish before the end of the year,' Brent answered sarcastically, then he picked up his design folio and made for his own rooms.

Ignoring his acrimonious mood, Faye went in search of Ana. She found her with the pigs, scattering rotting vegetable tops to supplement the animals' diet. Keeping her nose towards the breeze, Faye probed innocently, 'I didn't know we had a real live count living on our doorstep.'

'We didn't until yesterday,' Ana replied drily.

'You mean to say he's only just arrived?' Faye remarked, remembering the sly way the Conde had made out that he was an old neighbour. 'I suppose he's very rich?' she added dreamily.

'He squandered the family fortune in a matter of years,' Ana said in the true tight-lipped style of the peseta-conscious Majorcan. 'His house is in the hills across the valley, but nowadays he spends most of his time on the mainland.'

Recalling the feel of those warm lips on her hand, Faye asked musingly, 'Why do you suppose he's decided to return to the island?'

'I don't know,' Ana clapped the lid on the empty swill bin, 'but one thing you can be sure of—no good will come of it.'

Faye was amused at this gloomy forecast. The farm woman obviously had a low opinion of the Conde. As they made their way back to the courtyard she asked casually, 'This Carmina Flores. Is she a good friend of the Conde's?'

'They've known each other some years.' Ana flapped her apron at the menacing strut of the turkeys. 'It's understood that one day they will marry.'

Still glowing from the result of his attention to her, Faye said airily, 'It didn't look that way to me. I got the impression that the Conde has other ideas on the matter.'

Ana's blunt comment was an ominous one. 'Carmina has the hot blood of the Andalusian in her veins. She would kill rather than lose Enrique to someone else.'

Faye went off smiling to herself. Like all Spaniards, she thought, Ana tended to be a little melodramatic at times. She paid no attention to the clumsy note of warning in the woman's tones; her heart was far too taken up recalling the hidden promise in the Conde's gaze. And besides, Brent had shown that he resented the Conde's familiarity. It gave her a strange feeling of power to know that she had hit on something which got under *his* skin for a change.

Despite these feminine flutterings of Faye's concerning the Conde de Canyaret, she was not such a fool as to assume that all budding romances got off to such a whirlwind start. Why, she asked herself several times during the rest of that day, had the Conde suddenly decided to return to his house on the island? And why had he practically proposed to her at their first meeting?

She didn't have to wait long to find out.

The next day she was having a mild argument with Anofre and Ana over, of all things, the cows. Apart from the time when she had inadvertently bumped into one on the narrow strip of terrace, these beasts had been mere black and white shapes in the field behind the *finca*, or the source of plaintive mooings and shunting around in the cow shed. But on this occasion they were being driven to new pastures in the valley. As they passed through the courtyard Faye noticed to her horror that they were hobbled at the mouth, and could only walk by moving the chained right foreleg forward together with a swaying movement of their heads.

No amount of lecturing and explaining could convince the Rodriguez couple that this was a cruel practice. Cows were animals, weren't they? And how could animals have feelings? And anyway, if the beasts were given their freedom they would roam as far as Palma, and then where would the *señorita* be with her new-fangled ideas?

Trying to get through to Anofre was like chipping at a brick wall, and with his slow affable smile it was impossible to lose one's temper. All Faye could do was tell him that one day she would see that fences were erected on the land so that the cows could wander as they pleased. To this she got a reply to the effect that pampering was never intended for farm stock, but she went on arguing.

The slanging match in pungent Majorcan was on the wane when a vintage-style car, long and slightly battered in appearance, appeared round the slope of the cart track. As Anofre was just on the point of driving the cows down that way there developed something of an impasse, but the Conde, clasping a huge bunch of flowers in his hand, appeared to welcome the inconvenience.

Deftly picking his way from the car, he called to Carmina at the wheel, while rapidly increasing the distance between them, 'Back up a little, *carina*. I'll just go and pay my respects.'

How Carmina was expected to reverse all the way

back down the slope Faye couldn't imagine, and Anofre would be no help, she knew. But she was given no chance to witness the outcome of the muddle; the Conde contrived to whisk her away, and before she knew it they were on the narrow strip of terrace alongside the *finca*.

'For you.' With a flourish he presented her with the bunch of flowers, most of them the wild kind growing in the fields.

'Why, thank you!' Faye was overwhelmed. 'How very thoughtful of you ... er....'

'Enrique. At your service.' He bowed promptly and kissed her hand.

Faye met his wicked gleam with a thoughtful look. Yesterday it had been 'the Conde'. Today it was 'Enrique'. He was a fast worker all right!

With a dramatic display of feeling he inhaled the cool spring air. 'Ah, these April days! This air perfumed by the Mediterranean pines! What contentment is mine, living here amidst the outstretched arms of these hills and bays, these sun-kissed shores of my island home!'

'Ana told me you didn't arrive until the day before yesterday,' Faye said with a mischievous gleam.

Enrique eyed her unabashed. 'Nevertheless it is in my bones!' His glance became rooted on her. He continued rapidly in mystic tones, 'But what wild beauty can mute the radiance of an English flower ... the perfection of delicacy and expressiveness....' Faye's heart began to thump as he came closer. 'Those eyes ... like liquid amber ... And those lips ... just made for——'

'What are you telling her?' Carmina asked sharply from the gateway of the strip of terrace, panting slightly from her rush to join him.

Faye hadn't noticed until then that the Conde had switched from Spanish to Mallorquene during the conversation. She was so used to jumping from one language to the other when talking with Brent and the Rodriguez couple that the change meant nothing to her. But it was obvious that Carmina, being a main-lander, understood nothing of the island dialect.

Losing none of his coolness at her sudden appear-ance, the Conde replied blandly, 'Only how much we welcome her to our island, dearest.' After which he gaily turned his attention back to Faye.

Carmina watched them suspiciously as he viewed the land surrounding the *finca* and sighed theatrically. 'What wealth! What prosperity abounds here in these rolling wheatfields, these miles of vineyards and untold stretches of olive and almond groves!'

Faye was still swamped by his devastating charm. His fiery dark eyes were bright as he drew close to her. She didn't know what she expected as she stood there with him, looking out over the property of San Mateo; she just knew that she was neither surprised nor shocked when he murmured with a rakish gleam, 'It's not yours, and it's not mine, but together it could be ours.'

'Enrique! It's time we were going.' Carmina, watch-ing them sharply, tapped her foot impatiently.

'Coming, *querida*.' The Conde switched deftly back to Spanish. 'I was just telling Señorita Chalmers to feel free to call on us any time.' His gaze full of meaning, he encircled Faye with his arm, and bringing his head down beside hers he pointed to the distant blur among the trees. 'From here you can just see my humble abode.'

Carmina's breathing was becoming more pro-nounced, and the Conde turned amiable. 'As good neighbours we must perform the common courtesies. Is that not so, *carina*?'

Carmina was already moving off.

'*Adios*, Señorita Chalmers. Until we meet again.' Melting her with his fiery dark gaze, Enrique kissed Faye's hand and withdrew.

In a trance Faye stood and listened as his car started up. She heard it move out towards the lane entrance.

Her immediate reaction, once the spell was broken, was one mainly of amusement, though she couldn't deny a certain attraction when it came to the Conde's magnetic charm. When she thought about it, she had to admire his cool nerve and his blatant attempts to woo her.

Once he had discovered that he had been left nothing in her grandmother's will, he had obviously found out all he could about Faye, the sole benefactor. There was no doubt he had learned of the conditions of the bequest that Faye must marry locally, and was determined to waste no time in offering himself as the required Spanish suitor.

Faye strolled with a pleased look on her face. She liked the idea of having someone dangling for her attention, if only for the satisfaction of viewing the effect on Brent.

Her painting materials packed away for the day, she was making for the indoors across the courtyard when he drove in at the end of the afternoon. This secret knowledge gave her a sparkling exuberance as she purred in her usual barbed tones, 'Had a hard day on the fairway?'

'I've known better ones.' He climbed out of his car, watching her.

For some reason Faye felt unpleasantly conscious of the faded jeans hugging her curving hips and the old washed-out blouse too tight across her breasts. 'Never mind,' she smiled at him deprecatingly. 'Perhaps it won't be long before you're putting all those little green patches in their proper places.'

So saying, she tossed back her red-gold tresses and swung off carelessly towards the house, while Brent followed her with a narrowed, thoughtful gaze. Which was just how she wanted it.

CHAPTER SIX

Faye's reckless mood carried through until the following day, and on impulse she decided to pay a call on the Conde. Well, why not? There had been an open invitation in his eyes, and now that she had found something which rubbed the wrong way with Brent it might be interesting to pursue this line further. After all, *she* had to live with the galling knowledge that Brent spent most of his time with the Spanish beauties down at the golf course, didn't she?

She drew in her lower lip thoughtfully. There was Carmina, of course, but why should she worry about the fiery Andalusian woman? She had no claim on Enrique and he seemed perfectly happy to ignore her, so why shouldn't she, Faye, do the same?

Her mind made up, she dressed carefully in a short-sleeved, lightweight dress which had cost the earth in England. It was a vivid iris blue in colour, and the pale leather belt and buttons matched the hazel gold of her eyes.

It was a long time since she had taken such care with her appearance, and when she stepped outdoors towards her car, she was glad that she had made the effort. The afternoon was sunny and inviting, the air full of the tantalising messages of summer, and something else she couldn't put her finger on. She only knew that inhaling its magic was enough to increase the restlessness inside her. It felt good to have an excuse to go out visiting.

She had never driven down the steep winding cart track before, and as she crunched her way forward she felt a little terrified at the prospect. Ana, working in the courtyard, eyed the route she was taking with open distaste, and Faye smiled to herself at the woman's disapproval. Ana would never understand the subtleties and intrigues of modern society. Besides, the Conde was her neighbour. Why shouldn't she call on him if she wanted to?

Once down on to the floor of the valley, the driving was pleasant. The track, across to the main road which skirted the base of the pine-clad slopes, was pitted and rocky, but this was more than compensated for by the scenery. Familiar only with the bathing beaches and tourists spots on the island until her arrival at the *finca*, the Majorcan countryside was constantly offering new surprises for Faye. She had never before seen such carpets of green, not even in England, famed for its greenness.

And softening these undulating emerald stretches were the neat rows of slender almond trees heavy now with a different green plus the beginnings of fruit. Here and there the writhing grey trunk of an ancient olive; a tall clump of starry asphodel, added a fairy-tale touch to the scene. Driving through the green stillness with only the twitter of the birds somewhere in the clear soothing hue of the sky, one could almost expect to come upon a pixie reclining on a toadstool at any minute.

Up on the main road the illusion vanished. Building and construction lorries trundled busily by, bound for unknown destinations, and occasionally the short sharp sigh of air-brakes could be heard as some giant petrol tanker negotiated a bend in the road.

Faye's sympathies were with the cluster of houses which straggled over the hillside and hugged this busy highway, which had probably been no more than a leisurely market route for the farm produce carts a few short years ago. Keeping Enrique's residence in her sights, she prepared for the tortuous uphill climb along a winding stony track.

The engine of her little car wheezed asthmatically as she passed cobbled courtyards made gay by splashes of spring flowers and open doorways from whence came the usual powerful odours of garlic and spices.

The Conde's house was a rather dilapidated affair perched on the hillside overlooking the hamlet. Totally without character, it was simply an oversized barn-like cottage; its gaunt walls, Faye saw now, were washed in an ugly mustard colour. Once someone had tried to relieve the plain look of the windows along its front by framing them in white paint, which had turned grey with age.

To the sound of children's voices and yapping dogs, which came from a courtyard overgrown with prickly-pear cactus on the opposite side of the track, Faye parked her car and entered the wide opening between the encompassing stone walls of the mustard-coloured domain. Inside it was shabbily pretty, with remnants of a garden climbing up the hillside and pointing the way up to the doorway were little stone stairways and terrace walls holding an assortment of unkempt flower-pots.

Whether the Conde had seen her driving up from the main road she didn't know, but he came outdoors to greet her, perhaps a little flustered in his shirt sleeves and baggy trousers. As she approached his flippant dark gaze held a leaping light, as though he detected some purpose behind her visit, but Faye avoided making any comment on his conversation of the day before and turned her attention to the view.

'My goodness!' she exclaimed a little breathlessly, 'how lucky you are up here. I can see the *finca* way off in the distance across the valley. And what a marvellous uncluttered view of the mountain range!'

Enrique, rapidly concluding that this was no more than a social call, curved an arm deftly around Faye's waist and nodded with expansive approval on the scene. He barely gave her heart time to stop thudding at his touch before he explained with equal fervour, 'But we have a more delightful vantage point up at the top of the house. We will go and see it——now!'

More breathless than ever, Faye half regretted the wild impulse which had brought her here. The Conde was altogether too devastating in his approach. As he swept her along his black eyes flashing wickedly down into hers, and she laughed self-consciously, wondering if it was right to allow him to rush her indoors like this.

As they skirted the small elevated terrace and made for the open doorway, an unmistakable figure appeared below in the courtyard of the opposite house, plainly visible as one looked down from the terrace. Carmina, a squalling child on her hip, stood there in arrogant pose, taking note of everything that was going on. There was no doubt she had seen Faye's car parked outside on the track and was determined to keep her distrustful gaze trained on the Conde's house until Faye's departure.

They went indoors, and Faye was immediately struck by the chill air of the place. Like all Majorcan houses built for the scorching hot summers, it was colder inside, at this time of the year, than it was out.

Blind to almost everything but Enrique's nearness, she gathered blurred impressions of small rooms scantily furnished with whitewashed fireplaces and sheepskin rugs to warm the stone floors. Here and there, there were dusty reminders of the noble ancestry of the Conde in the form of oil paintings in heavy gilt frames, elaborate draperies embroidered and tasselled, and brown, yellowing photographs in silver filigree frames. But for all this faded glamour, the rooms wore an air of neglect.

The house seemed taller inside than it was out. They climbed and climbed up flights of stone steps, and at last reached a tiny *miramar*, a stone look-out balcony, built into an angle of the roof. The Conde unlatched the window which led out, and stepping through drew Faye forward to join him.

The view was so riveting that Enrique dimmed slightly against its magnificence.

Faye could see the cottages strewn down the hillside below the house and across, quite clearly, the track leading through the almond groves and up the opposite hillside to the *finca*. The valley was a patchwork of colour; the pale jade of ripening corn and sprouting beans; the red earth of newly ploughed stretches, dotted with the toy-like shapes of carob trees, tall stately cypresses and leaning pines.

But it was the views alongside the valley which enchanted Faye. Never had she been able to see the sea as it was now, a molten misty stretch across the plain on her right. And the mountains! At the *finca* one tended to forget them, catching glimpses only when one rounded the bend of the courtyard, or in between the trees and greenery. But up here they rose, towering, breathtakingly close, alongside one on the left, a range of craggy, brooding shapes, colossal and faintly mysterious in their splendour.

The Conde, delighted at her speechlessness, pointed to the two ochre-coloured bluffs in the mountain range, the same two that she was fond of painting. Colossal pillars of rock and earth crowned by sloping fringes of sparse greenery, they were like something out of an old Western movie in appearance. 'The left bluff. Can you see at the top?' Enrique drew closer to her, all the better to single it out. 'That's Alaró, the ruins of a Moorish stronghold. One day we will drive up there. The view from the castle, as you will see, surpasses all others.'

'Drive up?' Faye laughed her surprise. From what she could see, the tiny ruin in the sky seemed to be balanced precariously on the sloping edge of the bluff over the yawning canyon between. 'You surely can't get a car up there?'

'Almost to the top,' the Conde nodded. 'A twenty-minute climb on foot, and then....' He turned to fix her impishly with his velvet dark gaze. In his deep musical Spanish he had a way of talking which left her fighting for breath.

'And then ... what?' she laughed jerkily.

'And then ...' though the Conde spoke lightly, his words were like the thrilling ending of a beautiful song, 'you will find the whole world spread at your feet.'

Faye wished they could go downstairs. Her limbs were melting under Enrique's gaze; it didn't help to know that there was an artful gleam mingling with the magnetism in his dark eyes, a sharpness which searched for some sign of reaction in her to his daring proposal of yesterday.

Then, because he could read nothing in her face, he smiled his most disarming smile and spoke gaily. 'What a poor host I am. Come, we will drink together in the sunlight.'

Away from the close confines of the tiny look-out balcony and with a little breathing space between her and the Conde's hypnotic personality, Faye felt considerably more relaxed. They sat on one of the small elevated terraces outside the front door, where a white-painted table and chairs seemed to serve as an outdoor dining area.

From the kitchen quarters close by a bent, untidy figure resembling that of a manservant appeared. 'Bring the lady some of our best wine, Rafael. *Rapida-mente, por favor.*'

The sweeping arrogance with which he gave the order was, like everything about the Conde, just a little comic. Faye was willing to bet that the servant did exactly as he pleased most of the time, and judging by the dust in the rooms he was as slipshod in his work as he was in his appearance.

But she had no time to dwell on the mechanics of the Conde's household. The perfect host now, Enrique proved himself an entertaining companion as they sat together sipping a smooth *vino rosada*. He touched on a variety of subjects but without a great deal of seriousness, so that the conversation was riddled with laughter on both sides.

Faye was enjoying herself. The *finca* and Brent, with his disturbing blue gaze and mocking grin, felt to be a comfortable distance away. Sitting here basking in her budding friendship with the Conde, she no longer felt at the mercy of the man who could make or break her day simply by the way he looked at her.

The only thing that marred this merry interlude was the sultry Carmina's presence. She had positioned herself in the entrance of the opposite courtyard, facing the opening on to Enrique's property; in full view on their elevated terrace nothing of what Faye or the Conde did or said escaped her fiery, suspicious glare.

Though Enrique appeared blithely oblivious to the Andalusian woman's shadowy presence it obviously had an inhibiting effect on his expansive mood, for suddenly, on an impulse, he said, 'Let's go for a drive.'

'What, with two cars!' Faye sparkled her amusement.

'I'll bring you back and you can collect yours later.' Persuasive as ever, he took her arm, and before she could reply he had drawn her to the back of the house, where the low-slung vintage car was parked in a deserted side lane.

What Carmina must have thought when she heard the loud backfiring of the ancient engine and then a thunderous snort as they pulled away, Faye couldn't imagine. But with her hair blowing in her eyes in the open seat and the thrill of Enrique's rather reckless handling of the machine down the perilous slope to the road, she had little time to care.

They tore along the route circling the valley, through Caliséta, turning the villagers' heads as the Conde thundered through with the red-haired *chica* at his side. As they zoomed past the *finca* along the main road, Faye was delighted to see that their mad spin would take them directly alongside the new golf course only a few miles ahead.

The wind bit into her cheeks and the laughter on her lips was snatched away to go echoing across the fields, but she kept a sharp look-out for a familiar figure as they came up to the barren stretches dotted with machinery. There were several men working in the distance; any one of them could have been Brent. Faye secretly hoped that he was there somewhere. She didn't want her ride with the Conde to go unnoticed if she could help it.

All too soon, the churned-up stretches and banks of new greenery were curving away from the windscreen as they left La Zarzamora behind. The ancient engine under the long bonnet constantly snorted and bumped as though finished, then revived at the last moment with a new surge of power as they tore along a circular route encompassing farmhouses and villages and wild stretches of open countryside.

Eventually they joined the road coming in at the other end of the valley. After racing along it as though they were out to beat a train, they swung in at the little hillside hamlet, where the much-flogged car leapt and bucked up the stony track like a donkey with a bee in its ear, and finally came to a stop where they had started out, in the deserted lane behind the Conde's house.

When Faye drove her little car away ten minutes later there was no sign of Carmina in the courtyard of the house opposite. She gathered that the Andalusian woman had grown tired of waiting for their return.

After that afternoon Enrique became a regular visitor to the *finca*, dropping in once or twice a week on the pretence of motoring through to some other destination. It occurred to Faye that the Conde was sadly lacking in strength of character, for he never managed to call on her on his own. Whenever he put in an appearance in his dilapidated roadster, the arrogant and possessive Carmina was always glued to his side like a limpet to a rock.

However, Faye dropped in on the Conde now and then, and as she was employed in some kind of housekeeping capacity with the family across the way, Carmina was usually tied up with a bawling child or engaged in other household activities when she called. Undisturbed, Faye and Enrique could sit at the table on the terrace sipping wine and exchanging snippets of conversation. And when Carmina's hostile stare from the opposite courtyard became too penetrating, there was always the Conde's metal steed waiting out at the back to take them thundering and snorting through the village of Caliséta and out along the country roads.

On days like these Faye felt recklessly fulfilled. She wanted for nothing but the rush of the wind against her face, and the Conde, with all the gallant nature of the Spaniard, manoeuvring the wheel beside her.

But there were other days. Days when she spent her time working at the *finca*—or pretending to. She would sit at her easel waiting tensed up for the whisper of Brent's footsteps on the grass behind her, the sound of his car crunching in from the lane. She wanted to swing round on him, to flash her gaze tauntingly his way, wearing her friendship with the Conde on her sleeve so that he couldn't fail to notice it. But Brent never came near her these days.

Moodily she realised she missed his teasing remarks,

those moments he had set aside to stand watching her mockingly as she sat with paintbrush in hand, lingering, often though no words were spoken between them.

Sometimes she even planned it so she could be there in the courtyard, when he drove in in the afternoon. But though she did all she could to bait him with her new-found importance, Brent just eyed her with a peculiar ironic glitter, gave her a tight smile and proceeded on his way.

Faye felt curiously deflated by his behaviour. He gave her no opportunity to crow and it annoyed her. Hiding her pique behind her own little smile, she would go swinging off across the courtyard, tossing her flaming locks in a gesture of vainglorious indifference. Well, too bad if Brent didn't like the idea of being just a tenant at the *finca*—as far as she was concerned it felt good to have another man to turn to, if only to offset his supremacy around the place.

Brent's ironic disregard of her, coupled with Faye's high-flown independent mood, made life during those May days unbearable around the *finca*. The sun's heat increased and the sky was stained with the deep cloudless blue of summer, but conversation was limited between the tenant of San Mateo and its temporarily dispossessed owner.

Despite her tendency to strut on returning from an outing with the Conde, and the exultant glow in her eyes with which she met Brent's acrimonious blue gleam, Faye began to wish that something would happen to disperse the stifling feeling of tension that was mounting daily between them.

Release came unexpectedly one dark night when she had escaped from festivities taking place at the *finca*.

But it was Faye who was shattered by the outcome of her breathless confrontation with Brent.

CHAPTER SEVEN

FIESTA day on the island, as in all of Spain, is a time for great feasts and family get-togethers. As the Spanish calendar is littered with these local holidays, set aside to celebrate the birth of some revered saint, Faye had some experience of what went on at the *finca* on such occasions.

She had met Ana and Anofre's daughter Paloma, and Carlos her husband, and baby Carlitos and numerous other vague family connections and she knew a little of the frenzied preparations that took place on these festive days.

It so happened that the twenty-ninth of May was of special significance to the people of Caliséta, for it was from their village on that date centuries before that *un gran hombre* had sailed to far horizons and accomplished deeds which had gained him a place in the annals of Spanish history.

On the great day preparations began early at the *finca*. Members of the Rodriguez family descended, Ana's sisters among the first to arrive, for wasn't there much cooking to be done? Soon the little chimney in the cookhouse was belching smoke, and great slabs of pastry filled with home-made jam were handled in and out of the oven.

Everyone wanted to take part in this wild ritual of piling up food, for with the Majorcans the fun is in the work beforehand rather than the sitting down to the meal itself. All kinds of strange meats were chopped, ripped, sawn and flung into the cauldron bubbling over hot coals. There was a rich sauce to be prepared for the *caracoles*, snails gathered in a bucket on dark nights, days beforehand, and kept in readiness for the occasion.

Ana, falling over the chickens under her feet, rushed to and from the crackling fires in the cookhouse. Her sisters, hair flying and of the same wild countenance, crowded in with great bowls of messy food. Aunts and uncles, weighed down with piles of *sobrasada*, the spicy sausages, great round loaves and bundles of herbs, lent a hand, while the younger folk slopped water in and out from the well, and rushed in with fresh loads of firewood.

A tremendous strain was put on the oven, and there were frequent explosions. Miguel, the fifteen-year-old grandson of someone in the family, climbed manfully on to the roof of the cookhouse to see what the trouble was and made it infinitely worse by kicking the chimney loose from its socket. Sparks exploded right and left and roared in great clouds up to the sky. Members of the family fell through the doorway yelling advice from the ground while others laughingly disregarded the commotion and went on shouting (for Majorcans never talk) with their neighbour.

Each one did a wonderful job of hindering someone else, but there were no frayed tempers; everyone was having a wonderful time. Faye, standing a safe distance away in the farmhouse doorway, viewed the madness with undisguised amusement. The scene of the cheeky Miguel dancing with primitive abandon on the roof, the noisy inferno and still noisier shouts and gesticulations from the wild-looking mob down below, struck her as like something out of another age, the ruined *finca* and cluttered courtyard making an ideal setting for the medieval orgy.

The uproar subsided at mid-afternoon, when everyone succumbed to the heat; not from the raging oven but from the sun, which all Majorcans dread. But by early evening everyone was on the move again refreshed by swigs of wine and *bocadillos*, bread rolls the size of small loaves, sliced and filled with raw bacon or salted fish.

These *fiestas* were usually held indoors, but the night was warm and this was no small gathering. So, with great ceremony, Ana's best walnut table was carried outdoors, wedged allowing for the sloping surface of the courtyard and laid with a gleaming white tablecloth. The venerable members of the family were given the upright walnut chairs, while young and old after that made do with upturned buckets, old farm crates and anything else that might serve as a seat. Soon the table was groaning with food.

When Faye stepped out into the darkened courtyard her nose was assailed by all the weird and powerful cooking smells. Ana and Anofre were always pathetically pleased whenever she took a bite to eat with them; proudly they had included her in the festivities tonight. But Faye knew that her presence would merely be a token one, for much of what the Majorcans ate was far too explosive for her taste.

However, so as not to offend, and to show that she appreciated the invitation, she had taken special care with her appearance. Her cream silk dress, sleeveless and pleated from the waist, was patterned with tiny lilac flowers. She had put on lilac sandals, and a matching headband temporarily tamed her tumbling flame-gold hair.

There were cries of greeting as she approached the table. She was met by the sight of thrushes wrapped in cabbage leaves tied with string, which were a well-known delicacy locally but one which Faye could never take to, especially when she saw the dead birds strung up after slaughter outside the farmhouse door. Among other dishes, she recognised *frita Mallorquene*, square lumps of pig fat fried in deep oil, with vegetables, and *callos*, bits of tripe and entrails fried in oil. After that she curbed her gaze, deciding it might be wiser to concentrate on the friendly atmosphere pervading.

Happily, with the children romping around the table and the men wandering to and fro with glasses of wine in hand, it was possible to appear interested in the display of food without actually partaking much of it. She chatted to various members of the family and smilingly accepted the helpings of this and that which were eagerly thrust upon her.

Ana watched her anxiously. Though she knew a little of the English girl's ways, it was totally beyond her comprehension that these messy aromatic dishes might be considered by some as unappetising. And Faye wouldn't have hurt her feelings for the world. By scheming and working at it she managed to convey an impression of enjoying a taste of everything, which brought a gleam of satisfaction to the older woman's eyes, without doing more than nibbling at an olive on her plate or sipping from her brimming wine glass. An added comfort was the thought that the dogs, painfully thin and tethered pitilessly throughout their short lives, would come in for the greasy left-overs.

The table was lit for this special occasion by a brilliant *butano* lamp whose radiance illuminated the faces of the happy family group and spilled across the courtyard, defeated only by the shadows in the far corners. And into this light stepped the figure of Brent.

A roar of approval went up when he was spotted coming down the steps from his own apartment. It is the *señor*! *Salud*! Come and have a drink with us!

Faye's heart started to bump as she raised her gaze along with everyone else. Though she wouldn't have admitted it to a soul, least of all herself, a sudden ache of pleasure gripped her at the sight of him.

She knew that because today was a public holiday he had been confined to working in his rooms, and all day long this traitorous other half of her had been wondering if he would put in an appearance tonight. Well, he was here! And like her he had dressed for the occasion.

Her eyes lingered on the width of his shoulders in his cream wool shirt, the way its athletic cut made his tanned features look weatherbeaten and rugged. Pale slacks gave him a relaxed look despite their faultless tailoring.

To her consternation, everyone assumed that as he was a countryman of hers she would rush to perform the honours. A bottle of ice-cold *vino-espumoso*, Spanish champagne, was slapped into her hand, together with a glass with which to welcome and toast the *señor*. A laconic gleam in his blue eyes, Brent took the sparkling liquid from her unsteady grip and to the delight of everyone he bowed low in her direction before returning the toast.

From there, easy-going as always, he blended in effortlessly with the evening's festivities. As he spoke no Majorcan and some of the older members of the family knew nothing else, Faye was the link between his dry humour and the dour friendliness of the old folk.

Much laughter accompanied their bandying remarks and in her role as interpreter Faye found it difficult to keep her cloak of aloofness where Brent was concerned. She had the feeling that, close beside her, he knew this and was experiencing something of the same conditions himself.

But the Majorcans are a simple race, enjoying simple pleasures. Knowing nothing of the complicated intrigues of a more sophisticated society, their only concern tonight was in making the most of the *fiesta*, and *los Inglés* were their guests.

Faye in turn was aware only of Brent's presence. The smile he gave his listeners, white and even in his tanned features, played havoc with her emotions, she gave up trying to battle against heavy odds and let herself go in the party atmosphere. Brent, too, his shoulder brushing hers, his blue gaze fencing with her golden one at times, seemed to warm to the occasion.

Faye's cheeks burned a little with excitement. Laughter for the most part on her lips now, her head was nevertheless splitting in the pandemonium. Everyone was shouting above the clatter of crockery and food plates, the children romped, shrieked and whooped around the courtyard. While the dogs barking non-stop at their antics, Faye felt her voice getting fainter as she struggled to make herself heard.

When Brent was drawn into a conversation with Anofre and other male members of the family she knew she would have to get away. The Majorcans were the friendliest people on earth, but an hour or so in their volatile midst was more than enough for any outsider.

No one noticed her disappear into the shadows round the side of the cookhouse. Circling the hump of dark courtyard, she took the steep footpath that ran down alongside the *finca* into the valley. Out here in the soothing cool and quiet the stars hung down like lanterns in the sky. The line of mulberry trees were rustling black shapes against the milky glow. She turned into an opening below the tiered green terraces; here, half way down the hillside below the *finca*, was what must have been in the old days a kind of formal garden. All that remained now were the neglected ghosts of stately old trees, tattered shrubs and hedges and ornamental cactus which had grown wild with time.

But there was tremendous peace here. Faye had discovered this little oasis on one of her painting jaunts, and she liked to come here to escape from the farmhouse bustle of the courtyard. Now as she listened, all sounds from that area were shut off by the great bulk of the *finca* behind her.

She breathed deeply of the warm night air, laced with all the fragrance of the countryside. Soon it would be June, and already the winged crickets were rubbing their saw-toothed legs together in a symphony of sound. They favoured the cornfields, and as her eyes grew accustomed to the gloom she could make out the creamy-saffron stretches out in the valley and far beyond towards the mountains.

Eastwards on the flat horizon a huge orange moon was rising in phantom splendour. To Faye, watching the phenomenon out here, it was never just the moon —it was indeed another world. For as it floated eerily above the lip of the earth, breathtaking in its immensity, the shadowy etchings of its land and seas were clearly outlined against its muted copper glow.

She was witnessing its hushed arrival, sneaking up as if to pry on the sleeping earth, when a footstep sounded in the strip of garden. She knew at once it was Brent. He had followed her. Though her insides were strangely knotted up, every inch of her rejoiced in the knowledge.

An all-enveloping weakness made her lean against the nearby wall for support: in the gloom she could see the dark tan of his skin against his pale clothing, the carved line of his profile as he too gazed out at the view.

His presence was made conspicuous by his silence. For the past hour he had been the perfect companion, smiling and chatting alongside her amid the family group. Now all the old reservations were back. She even thought she sensed a kind of hard-bitten cynicism in his mood.

When he spoke at last his words had a twisted, banal ring. 'Quite a sight, the old moon hung out there. A couple of Spanish guitars in the background and who knows what we might get up to.'

A few feet away, Faye was aware only of her pulses pumping uncomfortably, and did not reply.

'Stars too, tonight. And the smell of summer.' He sniffed appreciatively. 'Great night for a stroll. And the best part to come.'

Whatever that meant! Faye had a feeling he was taunting her in some way. He turned on her without warning, but his tones still held their pseudo-light quality as he grinned tightly at her, 'You know, they do say you can read a newspaper by the brilliance of the Majorcan moon.'

'I wouldn't know about that,' Faye managed at last with the same false flippancy.

'We'll have to try it some time. I'm sure there's a lot of truth in it,' Brent concluded with a twisted smile.

Now that he had established a footing for conversation he seemed, like her, to be feeling his way. He stood for some time before searching for cigarettes, then flicked his lighter under one and inhaled deeply, breathing the smoke out long and leisurely. He asked with a kind of steely control, 'How's the Spanish boyfriend?'

'Oh, in the pink!' Faye replied. She was beginning to sound as banal as he was. And remembering the luscious girls billeted in the villa beside the golf course she asked with feline smoothness, 'And how are the English lessons?'

'Oh, going great guns!' Brent grinned crookedly.

From there the crickets took over. Even if she had been able to think of another clever remark, Faye's voice had deserted her again. She felt as though she was walking a tightrope, flimsily constructed, and about to give way at any moment.

The throbbing of her pulses seemed to drown out the sounds of the night. She knew she would have to get away or suffocate from their wild hammerings.

She whirled round, but before she could take more than a step away Brent's hand snaked out to catch her wrist. 'Going so soon?'

Beneath his taut smile she could sense the leashed violence in him. It forced her to reply in high-pitched quivering tones, 'We seem to have exhausted our supply of conversation.'

'Who needs to talk?'

She had time only to glimpse the smouldering blue of his eyes as he jerked her against him. The feel of his lips on hers opened the floodgate of longing, yearning for his touch which she knew now she had craved for so long. As his arms strained her close she melted in the blaze of fulfilment, too weak to know anything but the easing of this insatiable hunger. Everything was hers for the taking. Everything.

Quiescent against him, she might have gone on soaring in the starry paradise of his kiss if she hadn't suddenly awakened to the savageness of it. No, not just savageness in his rough handling of her, in his bruising of her lips, but ... yes, she was sure of it ... contempt!

As quickly as she had succumbed to his embrace she fought wildly to escape it. Holding her in a vice-like grip, Brent looked at her with an odd smile as she strained from his roaming lips. 'What's wrong? Is it the colour of my eyes that doesn't fit? Perhaps if I changed my name to Alvarez or Gomez ... ?'

Struggling, Faye panted close to him, 'You can't expect me to know what you're talking about.'

'Oh, come now!' Brent's smile was edged with frost. 'Don't tell me your eager little ears aren't tuned in the right direction. You need a Spanish husband if you're going to get what you want—San Mateo. It looks like this Conde guy happened along at just the right time, doesn't it?'

So that was what he thought! The shock was like a body blow to Faye. Woman-like, she had wanted to goad him into noticing her. Oh yes, she had fooled herself into believing that she enjoyed the Conde's company, but she knew now that she had encouraged his friendship solely to annoy Brent. She had wanted to make him just the teeniest bit jealous, but somehow everything had gone wrong. He actually believed she was out to snare the Conde in order to get her hands on San Mateo. He dared to think that she would stoop to something as low as scheming towards a marriage of convenience.

She was staggered at the way his mind had worked. Well, if that was what he thought of her, she had no intention of disillusioning him now! The mere idea of it whipped up a seething fury within her.

In that moment she loathed him with all the hate that goes hand in hand with loving, and she wanted only to hurt him as he had hurt her. She flung up her head and flashed at him, 'Hasn't it occurred to you that I might want the Conde for himself?'

'No, that hadn't occurred to me.' Brent's blue eyes burned ironically into hers.

Too late she knew she had given too much away in her kisses. Angry with her own weakness and with him for knowing what he did, she wanted only to wipe that self-satisfied look off his face.

Her hand came up. She aimed it with all the force she could muster and blazed at him shakily, 'Well, perhaps this will convince you!'

Brent countered the blow in mid-air. His fingers clamped around her wrist as he said with his blue glint, 'Save the strong-arm stuff for later. We live under the same roof, remember.'

Though his expression was sardonic a tiny flame flickered in his gaze; panting and helpless, Faye stayed pinned against him. In the skirmish she had lost her headband. Now her thick red hair tumbled about her face and shoulders and in the all-revealing moonlight her heavy-lashed hazel eyes were liquid bright, and with her straight pert nose, and wide soft mouth she looked as she ached to look at this moment, lovely and desirable.

She could feel Brent's heart thudding against her own. His blue eyes above hers darkened to pinpoints of fire; if he had brought his mouth down on hers then she would have given herself to him completely, despite her anger. His fingers sank into her flesh. Then at the last moment, with a gleam of distaste in his eyes, he slackened his hold and drawled, 'Give my regards to the Conde when you see him.'

Faye was still tense, waiting for his kiss—if he had wanted to make her feel cheap and scheming, he couldn't have planned it better. She read a world of meaning in his look, but the hardest to take was his contempt.

Smiling back at him, she met it with all the searing scorn that his rebuff had kindled in her, then she swung away towards the path up to the house and left him to the moonlight.

Well, let him think she wanted the Conde and San Mateo. She'd rather die now than tell him he was wrong!

CHAPTER EIGHT

June brought many changes at the farm. The roar of machinery could be heard as a combine harvester worked in the wheat fields and tractors carted away bales of straw, and Anofre was full of grumbles at having to pay the astronomical figure of a thousand pesetas an hour for mechanised assistance. The vines needed trimming, and the beans still had to be picked, but he couldn't afford to pay the wages the men were asking in the village. He and Ana and their two elderly hired hands spent all their waking hours working in the fields.

The sheep were relieved of their heavy coats of wool in a painstaking manner. Each one was clipped, slowly and laboriously, with a pair of ordinary shears, down in the shade of the fig orchard. They were shut away all day now in the big tumbledown shed at the foot of the slope in the valley, and around eight o'clock at night, when the harmful rays of the sun had diminished, Tomás the crippled shepherd could be heard shouting instructions to his dog as the sheep were herded out to graze during the dark hours. They no longer passed through the courtyard in the mornings, and to Faye it was a relief not to be wakened at dawn by their noisy, clanking bells.

She moved about listlessly these days. There were pale lilac shadows under her eyes and a pallor about her skin which some might have put down to the heat, for it was true the summer days were everything she could have wished.

The island now with its shimmering colours, its cobalt blue skies and violet and sage mountains, this was the Majorca she knew and loved. And yet she could feel no spark of joy at her surroundings, nothing.

She had had no real conversation with Brent since their stormy embrace that night in the garden. They spoke to one another in a fashion as they passed in the courtyard, or met in the old lean-to shed beside their cars, but Brent's smile was always twisted when he looked at her and Faye hid the raw ache inside her beneath a veneer of cool unconcern.

She knew now how it was with her and Brent. She had loved him for so long without knowing it, or if she had known it she had tried to stifle her feelings beneath her resentment of his presence at the *finca*. The realisation brought her no joy now, only black despair. Brent had made it only too clear what he thought of her.

The Conde called on her often. He regarded her pale subdued look as a sign that she was weakening towards him, and proceeded carefully despite his underlying excitement. He had a charm, a sensuality that could beat down the defences of any woman, but there was nothing deeper in it than that, and Faye knew it.

Brent was always the perfect host whenever he was around. He greeted Enrique warmly in the courtyard, and brought out chairs from the farmhouse so that everyone could sit in the cool shade. He even had a way with Carmina, compelling her to remove her burning gaze for brief moments from Enrique while he chatted pleasantly with her, or walked.

But Faye wasn't fooled by his suave exterior. She knew what his thoughts were as he watched her in the company of the Conde, and whenever his blue gaze clashed with hers, beneath the hard glint of amusement, she caught the full force of his distaste.

Often on these occasions she couldn't help thinking how unfair life was. From the start it had been the Conde who had chased *her*. And it was *he* who had put the veiled proposition of marriage to *her* so that she could inherit San Mateo. But what was the point of going into all that now? Even if she told Brent he wouldn't believe her. And in a way she supposed she had brought it on herself. She knew now that in playing up to the Conde she had simply wanted to make Brent come running. What a fool she had been not to realise that he saw her as nothing more than an opportunist!

She had brought it on herself, but in her heart of hearts she couldn't forgive Brent for thinking the worst of her. And her hurt made her fiercely independent. Not for anything would she let him see that she needed his love.

Her work suffered. She could find no zest to paint the scenes that were crying out to be put on canvas; the beautiful rose-glow of the sunsets, the lengthening shadows across the land in the red-gold light of evening.

She was making a half-hearted attempt to sketch the Mexican cactus on the upper terrace alongside the south wall of the *finca* one afternoon when the sound of a car pulling into the courtyard scattered what little concentration she had managed to scrape together. Drat! More visitors. How was a body expected to get any work done around here? Reluctantly she rose from her easel. She supposed she had better go and see who it was.

By the time she had skirted the house and climbed the path up to the courtyard Brent was there, shaking hands with Bart Templeton. Greta looked brilliant in peacock blue slacks and sun top, sparklingly incongruous amid the rough stone surroundings. She waved gaily when she saw Faye, and said drily to Brent, 'We heard you were out this way. We would have come sooner, but we've only just washed off the paint of winter decorating.'

Brent was wearing rough linen slacks and brown sports shirt. He looked casual and relaxed and as always the sight of him drove a skewer of pain into Faye's heart. He said, tossing his tight grin her way, 'Meet my landlady.'

'We're old friends.' Greta hugged Faye, her silken eyebrows arching upwards in her beautifully made-up face as she added, 'Didn't she tell you? We met on the ferry coming out from Barcelona.'

Brent let his gaze rest on Faye, and said with that suggestion of a curl to his smile, his tones laced with sardonic humour, 'We don't indulge much in social chat.'

Faye avoided his gaze. Her throat was too tight to make a reply. She felt Greta's discerning gaze on her, raking her pale face and shadowed eyes, and knew that she had sized up the situation at a glance.

Smiling over the tumult inside her, Faye greeted Bart, impeccable as ever in tailored summer suit, college tie and pastel-coloured shirt. Unlike his wife he was blissfully oblivious to the strained atmosphere. 'My favourite girl!' He opened his arms to Faye. She moved in and let him drop a kiss on her cheek. Slender in cotton dress, she had tied her hair into a coil on one shoulder for coolness. He held her away from him and grinned, 'You're looking adorable. Fragile as a summer rose.'

Faye gave a little laugh as though she hadn't a care in the world. She felt fragile all right and the sight of Brent's smile didn't help. She knew that Greta has seen it too; the Conde appeared on the scene at just the right moment.

Faye had been wondering how she was going to cope with the tense situation between her and Brent when the racy old car came roaring and wheezing its way up the cart track from the valley. Enrique, looking quite debonair in white hip-hugging trousers and striped shirt, his shaggy hair trimmed to the edge of his collar, strode over to greet her. 'Faye, my dear!'

Carmina, stiff and formal as a lacquered doll in her bottle-green frilled dress, her scraped-back hair oiled and shining like black glass, followed him briskly into the courtyard.

Faye made the introductions between the Templetons and the Spanish couple, and for a while everyone stood around and chatted politely. Brent had rigged up a table to go with the chairs outside the farmhouse doorway, and Faye hurried away to fetch a tray of drinks. When she returned Greta was brightly polishing up her Spanish with Carmina, discussing the cattle ranches on the Andalusian plain.

The men talked together, but Enrique detached himself when Faye appeared. With his flashing dark eyes, warm with succinct humour, and the way he had of making her feel every inch a woman, Faye had to admit it felt good to drown her hurt in his attentions. She knew that Brent watched her with his acrimonious gleam, but she knew too that part of her wanted to hurt him as he was hurting her. So she behaved most charmingly towards Enrique. From time to time, as he reciprocated with his own particular brand of charm, she saw Greta eyeing him in a speculative way.

When the drinks were finished Brent offered to take Bart up to his rooms to show him the work he had been doing on the golf course sketches and designs. As they went Greta suggested playfully alongside Faye, 'How about showing me the haunted ruins?' Then realising that this might appear rude she turned to look back. 'Oh, but there are your other guests.'

Though she had spoken in English, Carmina seemed to get the gist of what she had said, for she assured them in her harsh Spanish, 'Please don't worry. Enrique and I will be perfectly happy to sit here until you return.'

The Conde, never very good at asserting himself when Carmina spoke in those tones, sat down indolently to smoke a cigarette.

As they made for the flight of stone steps Faye said, pretending lightheartedness, 'Well, what do you think of my fabulous inheritance?'

Greta looked around the uneven courtyard and wrinkled her nose delicately at the farm smells lingering on the hot air outside the tumbledown sheds. 'Well,' she murmured dryly, 'I suppose you could say it has a quaintness.' She stopped to fondle the black shape who had stirred himself lazily in her passing. 'Hello,

113

brute, what are you doing there?'

'That's his home,' Faye nodded wryly at the dog's stone shelter cemented against the side of the house. 'Don't ask me why he spends his time chained there. Like all the rest,' she waved an arm at the other small shelters around the courtyard, 'he must serve some useful purpose around here, but I'm not sure what it is.'

'The Majorcans have some odd ways, poppet,' Greta replied. 'Yet you usually find they know what they're doing.'

'I know,' Faye quipped. 'I let the dogs loose every morning, but after sniffing around for a while they always come back to their own spots.'

'Well, there you are!' Greta reasoned. They both laughed as they climbed the steps.

Faye's humour dried on her lips when she passed through into the huge dim salon. She hadn't been up here since that night Brent had caught her in his arms when she had fled from the ghostly happenings in a bedroom. Her heart twisted painfully inside her when she recalled that moment now.

She felt his presence in the shadowy interior, was alive to all that was masculine here, the whisper of cigarette smoke on the air, the merest suggestion of the fragrance of after-shave lotion. So many more intangible things that told her this was where Brent spent a good deal of his time.

They passed by the open doorway of his rooms as Faye led the way towards the opposite entrance. Greta eyed her surroundings with interest, the sombre portraits and dusty drapes. She was gigglingly intrigued as they traversed creaky corridors and climbed eerie staircases, clutching Faye's arm at the slightest rustle of sound, and peering into rooms whose atmosphere had remained undisturbed for centuries.

'Ooooh!' she gasped as she crept past shadowy shapes

in the hallways. 'You don't mean to tell me you came up here in the *dark*!'

Faye nodded and smiled. 'This is where I tried to sleep once.' She opened the door into the small L-shaped room. Apart from the dust and the hot, inured smell of rotting beams the room appeared perfectly normal. 'It was probably all my imagination,' Faye said lightly, walking between the beds and glancing out into the little courtyard where the greenery was thriving under a hot blue sky. 'On a winter's night with the rain pouring and the wind howling, it's easy to frighten oneself into thinking all sorts of things.'

'Don't you believe it, ducky.' Greta gazed about her at the inanimate objects. 'There's *things* here, I can feel it. I wouldn't sleep up here for all the gold in Fort Knox.'

Faye's smile drooped a little wryly. She had no intention of repeating the experience, but with her it wasn't a fear of the unknown now. It was the fear of the power of her love for Brent which kept her from wandering in this section of the house at night.

It was Greta's nature to be perceptive. She had noticed the unhappy light in Faye's eyes, the lethargy in her manner. As they made their way back to the main salon she probed innocently, 'What's it feel like, sharing the house with a super golf course designer?'

'Brent is just a tenant here,' Faye replied stiffly. Still raw and aching after her clash with him, she found the subject of their fight too painful for discussion.

Greta's blue eyes were not without a certain twinkle, but she was shrewd enough to leave well alone in this direction. Instead she made a pretext of studying a crumbling wall tapestry in passing, and commented idly, 'The Conde's quite a dish.'

'He is rather nice,' Faye smiled. Despite his ulterior motives she didn't dislike Enrique.

Greta noted her reaction, and it puzzled her. She

hadn't a hope of knowing what was going on. Giving up, she mentioned as a sly afterthought, 'And Carmina. Is she a friend of the Conde's too?'

'Yes, they've known each other for years. Why do you ask?'

'No reason!' In her dry way Greta was all wide-eyed and noncommittal. Then she tossed in negligently, 'She just looks as if she'd like to slit your throat, that's all.'

'Carmina's all right,' Faye gave her a wan smile. 'Just a bit possessive, that's all.'

As they crossed the salon she could hear Brent talking to Bart from somewhere just inside his doorway. Dreading running into him up here, she said hastily, with forced gaiety, 'And now you must come down and see my den and my paintings.'

Greta, not the dumb blonde she was often made out to be, accepted briskly and made a discreet exit. Faye, she noticed, had paled visibly at the sound of Brent's voice.

Downstairs in the farmhouse, she eyed Faye's work of the past four months with critical indecision. 'Hmm! They're good ... quite good. . . .'

'But not earth-shattering,' Faye said wryly, voicing her own anxieties.

'Well, what paintings are these days?' Greta hedged. 'And anyway, you've got a nice sense of colour, and that's what the tourists like, lots of colour.'

Faye had to be satisfied with that. She quickly dispensed with the line of pictures while Greta wandered about the room, viewing the cathedral-like heights of the ceiling and the stained beams contrasting darkly with the whitewashed surround. 'I bet it's lovely and cool in here in the summer,' was her way of highlighting the best of the fairly primitive arrangements.

When they went out into the courtyard the two men had returned and joined the others, and all were chatting amiably together, drinks in hand. Even Carmina, possibly because she had been left so long in the Conde's company, seemed in a better mood.

When her glass had been refilled, Greta attached herself to Brent and teased him with an affection born between friends of long standing. 'Tell me, you gorgeous brute,' she linked an arm through his and eyed him with a challenging sparkle, 'when are we going to start painting the town, like we used to do on the Costa del Sol?'

Brent grinned, though there was a tightness in his manner as he drawled, 'I'm getting too old for those kind of capers, Greta.'

'Come off it!' she scoffed. 'It's only three years since you and I danced in a barrel of olives at the *fiesta del Carmen.*' Gigglingly she leaned close to him. 'Do you remember that night?'

'Will I ever forget it?' Brent winced goodnaturedly. 'Get her off me, Barton.'

Watching the two of them spar playfully Faye would have given anything to be in Greta's shoes, to have Brent as close as he was to her knowing there was no bitterness or irony between them. But because this was never likely to be she stayed close to the Conde as Greta went on ribbing him. 'There's fun to be had on the coast, honey chile. We've got the sea on the doorstep and every known drink in the bar, and anyway....' Afraid she was getting nowhere, she confronted him dazzlingly, 'We're giving the first dance of the season on Saturday night, and Faye and the Conde and Carmina,' she tossed out the invitations recklessly, 'are all invited, so you can't duck out. Tell him, Bart.'

'You know us, old chap,' Bart tilted his glass. 'We're in the business, so why not enjoy it? And incidentally,' his brown eyes gleamed with that rapport that exists only between men, 'the hotel's loaded with beautiful girls.'

Brent's blue glance clashed fleetingly with Faye's, then he said with a grin, the meaning of which she was not meant to miss, 'Since you put it like that ... how can I refuse?'

Faye was torn between anger and tears. When it came to beautiful girls she had seen Brent in action. Hadn't she been tormented by the memory of the opulent villa beside the golf course and its glamorous occupants, ever since her visit? Consumed by red-hot jealousy at the implications of his reply, she put her arm in Enrique's and gave him an answering knife-edged smile. 'The Conde and I would love to come.'

'And Carmina, of course,' Greta switched to Spanish so that the other two would know what all the talk was about.

Carmina accepted the invitation to the dance a little coldly, as though she sensed she had been included as an afterthought, but the Conde was more appreciative. He dropped a hand warmly over Faye's and breathed, '*Queridissima mia.*'

Good old Enrique! He could always be relied upon to embellish an occasion with his Spanish gallantry. Faye clung to him, knowing that Brent had heard his words of endearment. She saw his twisted smile as he turned to talk to Bart and she knew she had scored a victory.

The conversation was fairly general after that, until Carmina told Enrique they would have to be going. As he hurried to do her bidding, the Templetons took their leave also. Faye made a show of waving the Conde off down the cart track, then disappeared rapidly indoors before Brent returned from seeing the Templetons off.

She felt drained from her emotional battles with him and was in no hurry to come face to face with him again.

CHAPTER NINE

Faye's immediate worry, once she had recovered sufficiently after the jolt her heart had suffered, was her rapidly dwindling finances. By living frugally these past few weeks and shopping only for what she couldn't possibly do without, she had managed to spin her savings out to the maximum; but now she was running out of clever ideas, and anyway there were none that could be applied to an empty bank account.

Sitting down in her room one day with a book of figures, she arrived at the frightening realisation that, even going very carefully, she would be completely penniless in three weeks. Maybe less!

She had her paintings, thank heaven. The holiday season was well under way, and it was obvious now that there was no time to be lost in putting her plans for an earned income into action. Though she spent little time in Llosaya, dropping in only for her weekly supermarket requirements, she had noticed the increase in tourists in the town.

The next morning she piled her pictures in the back of the car and drove away. It was one of those faultless summer days that happen only in Majorca. The sky, pale and clear, was still washed with the cool of early morning; with no wind as yet to ripple its surface, the countryside stood etched in the stillness, its greenery caught here and there by the first slanting rays of golden sunshine. For the birds it was a time of rejoicing, and every one gave voice to the morning in a twittering crescendo of sound.

Faye drove slowly, with the car windows open, loving the feel of the breeze brushing her hair, and pushing all thoughts of starving in her back room at the farmhouse to the furthermost corners of her mind.

But her struggling optimism dropped and sank like a stone when she reached Llosaya. As she drove through the tourist areas, gay with holidaymakers and coach parties enjoying their first stop outside Palma, she was shattered at what she saw. Every street corner, every *calle* entrance, disused doorway and shopping arcade, was lined with artists' pictures. Oil paintings depicting the same scenes and subjects that she had chosen, and most executed with far greater skill.

There were dozens of farmhouse cockerels, and scenes of almond trees, writhing olives and purple mountain ranges met one at every turn. Faye viewed them all in a depressed state of mind, her pride in her own talent taking a distinct header in the face of all this competition. Her parents had indulged her in an art education and the other members of her family had always been full of well-meaning praise, but away from the comforting bosom of such encouragement she was beginning to realise that it was a cold hard world.

She drove to the showrooms in the heart of town and found they were plastered in the same way. However, she had to eat, so she left a few pictures with each gallery and agreed to pay a small percentage on any picture sold, for the privilege of displaying her work. Watching as her efforts were arranged around the walls, she was glumly aware that there was nothing but the flair of her signature in one corner *F. Chalmers*—as regards subject anyway—to distinguish her paintings from so many others.

After this latest blow, she was in no mood to rush back to the *finca* to churn out more 'works of art', nor dared she do any food shopping. Supposing she never sold a picture! The thought made her go weak at the knees. Though she could ill afford it, she would have to splurge on a drink, and sit down before she collapsed out of sheer fright.

The plaza lay broad and shining beneath the sunlight. Loungers sprawled in the shadows beneath the vivid green trees and in the deep stone arcades which edged the open square morning coffee drinkers clad in cool summer garb lolled at the café tables.

Faye sank down thankfully and ordered *café con leche*. She tried to soothe her troubled mind by watching the fountain running with water in the centre of the plaza, and the continual procession of passers-by; women carrying large clay amphoras on their hips, and men pushing barrow-like frameworks piled high with local pottery. Tourists were happily snapping their cameras outside the shops and cafés painted in gay colours and brilliant in the sunshine; plump couples marched beneath the trees, a string of neat and clean offspring in tow.

She didn't notice the familiar figure hurrying in by the crowd, short legs supporting a fat, round middle and close-cropped grey hair standing up slightly on the crown.

It was Don José Andrés who saw Faye, and halting greeted her effusively. '*Señorita Chalmers! Como esta?*'

'*Muy bien, gracias,*' she took his outstretched hand. '*Y usted?*'

'*Muy bien.*' The greetings over, he eyed her smilingly but with a look of piercing conjecture. Then he suggested urbanely, 'May I join you? It is so pleasant to sit and while away one's time over a drink, is it not?'

Faye was sure he had been hurrying to an appointment, but he seemed keen now on the idea of taking a seat, so there was not much she could do to deter him. He ordered an *anis* for himself and paid for her coffee as well, at the same time enquiring jovially about her welfare and how she had been faring at the *finca* since last they had met.

She tried to give a rosy enough picture, although they both knew that San Mateo offered little more than rustic comforts. When the subject of her settling in at the farmhouse with the Rodriguez couple had been exhausted, José Andrés examined the syrupy liquid in his glass and said with a mischievous gleam, 'You are finding the Conde de Canyaret a fascinating personality. Am I right?'

Faye felt her cheeks turn red, and resentment at José Andrés' tone of voice made her reply a little coolly, 'We're good friends, yes.'

'The man's a wastrel, and neither his breeding nor the family fortunes, long since squandered, have managed to curtail his appetite for spending,' the lawyer said bluntly. 'On the other hand, I can see the reasons for your interest in him. He is of course of pure Spanish blood, and the only stipulations your grandmother made were....'

Not him too! 'Señor Moreno,' Faye cut across his smiling assumptions with quivering precision, 'may I say that you seem remarkably well informed concerning my activities of late.'

'We have our own island grapevine, Señorita Chalmers,' José Andrés shrugged mildly. 'You have been seen often in the company of the Conde these past weeks. That makes news in a tiny community like ours, especially in the villages in the area where a marriage between the Conde and Carmina del Flores has been long assumed.'

Faye found it difficult to conceal her annoyance. She retorted, struggling to keep her tones normal, 'As far as I know the Conde is a free man, with a mind of his own. I'm sure neither he nor I wish to have our lives dictated by village gossip.'

'True,' José Andrés nodded, again giving her that knowing smile which set her teeth on edge. 'And while I agree that it is important for you to make a marriage which will entitle you to the wealth of San Mateo, I would ask you to tread carefully, my dear. Carmina del Flores has Andalusian fire in her veins. You might find her a dangerous rival should you declare open war on the territory she has long since come to regard as her own.'

'I'm sure the Conde can handle Carmina,' Faye said abruptly. 'And now if you will excuse me, Don José,' she rose from the table, 'I have a lot of shopping to do.'

'Of course.' José Andrés finished his drink. 'I too have an urgent appointment.' He rose hurriedly and shook her hand, his sunny gaze piercing the screen of her hauteur to try and assess the effect of his little talk.

Faye gave away nothing of the icy fury seething inside her until José Andrés had become lost in the bustle of the plaza. Then storming away to pick up her car, she gave vent to her feelings as she tore out of the town in a cloud of dust.

It seemed that everybody regarded her as nothing more than an opportunist. Not only Brent, but the lawyer and probably Carmina too. And the surrounding villages were rocking with the news of her friendship with the Conde. Well! She swung the wheel viciously along the country roads. She might take them all at their word one day. She was practically penniless, all she needed was a Spanish husband and her financial problems would be over. Enrique would marry her tomorrow if she wanted it. She had only to say the word.

Eyes bright with angry tears, depressed at the way things were going, she accelerated blindly, feeling reckless and in the mood for anything.

Faye's raw and bruised feelings had no time to heal before Saturday, the night of the dance at the Templetons' hotel. It seemed that the Conde was her only friend, and it was with him in mind that she dressed for the occasion.

She possessed a dress of white chiffon, its strapless bodice crossed with a scarf of sugar-pink. Though she was quite happy to slop around in jeans and shirt she could wear a dress when it suited her; and tonight, she told herself with grim satisfaction, it suited her very well. To offset the bareness of her arms and shoulders she fastened a silver necklace around her neck with a jewelled pendant which nestled in the hollow between her small breasts.

She had taken care with her make-up, and chose a frosted pink lipstick to go with the pink on her dress. Far from clashing with the auburn radiance of her hair, the two blended to give a subdued effect, and with a white chiffon headband that showed the smooth lines of her face to advantage, she looked outwardly serene at least. Liberal use of her precious rose-scented perfume completed her toilet.

Outdoors it was warm enough to manage with no more than a lace stole draped round her shoulders. The summer nights were long now. The sky, with that clear-washed, steely-blue look of evening, was pierced here and there with the largest and brightest of stars. From the knoll of the courtyard it was still possible to see the countryside spread out below. Clothed in the light mantle of twilight, every square inch throbbed and trilled with the insects of the night.

Faye waited anxiously for the Conde's car to appear up the track from the valley. No arrangements had been made for the trip to the coast, but she assumed Enrique would call and pick her up before starting out. She was keen to get away before Brent appeared, but she had been out of doors for little more than a minute when he strolled out from the lean-to shed which served as a garage.

He was dressed for the evening. Her hungry gaze soaked up that much before she could stop it. In a dark lounge suit his shirt was a brilliant stab of white in the gathering shadows, but no more so than the crooked smile he gave her as he approached.

She saw the glitter in his blue eyes as he viewed her; his gaze trailed with mocking appraisal over the bare curve of her shoulder beneath the lace stole, lingered on the plunging neckline of her dress. 'The Conde's a lucky man,' he grated, coming close to her. 'I wonder if he knows what goes on behind that ice-cool exterior?'

Faye felt the life-draining antagonism twisting in her insides. 'Why don't you tell him?' she asked acidly.

'And destroy a beautiful illusion? Not me!' Brent's grin was tight with meaning. 'I feel bad enough having already poached on his preserves. How about you? You must have some regrets about your *faux pas* the other night.' His derisive blue gaze flamed into hers. 'Or are you still game for what you can get on the side?'

Her heart pounding at his nearness, Faye choked, 'Sometimes I find you insufferable!'

'But only sometimes!' With that odd grin Brent jerked her against him before she could protest. His mouth came down roughly and moved tantalisingly close to hers. But knowing how she yearned for his kiss, he kept his lips just a heartbeat away, exploring the bare regions of her throat, the velvet lobes of her ears.

Faye found herself melting in his arms. Every part of her craved for his love, but Brent like this, sneering and contemptuous—no!

She stiffened and fought off his kiss. 'Brent, let go of me! Brent—please—there's a car coming!'

'So there is!' His voice shaking, Brent drew away sardonically just before the headlights of the Conde's car flashed round into the courtyard.

In a state of confusion, Faye had no time to gather her widely scattered emotions before Brent was strolling across the courtyard and speaking to Enrique and Carmina breezily. 'You two go ahead. I'll give Faye a lift in my car.'

As Carmina was at the wheel the response in getting the dark thundering shape out towards the main road was immediate, and in the stillness left behind with only the smell of exhaust smoke in her nostrils Faye stood and fumed while Brent went lazily to back out his car. He reversed alongside her, but she shook off his assistance as he tried to help her into her seat.

It wasn't just that his embrace had aroused all, which, until she had known the feel of his lips, had lain dormant in her. What angered her more was that she had lacked the will to resist him—a fact which, in his present mood, must have given him ironic satisfaction.

They drove to Porto Cristo in strained silence. Faye didn't know why Brent had chosen her company—he couldn't be enjoying it any more than she was his. Her heart ached when she thought of her true feelings submerged beneath the layers of hurt and misunderstandings. She would have given anything to be back on the old footing with him. Even the half-fighting, teasing relationship they had known in the early days was better than this.

The cove of Porto Cristo was a twinkle of fairy lights as they approached from the inland route. The town itself, wrapped in the warm soft air of summer, was alive with briefly-dressed, sun-flushed holidaymakers, touring the sights among the bright lights, lounging at café tables now pleasantly cool under the stars. The water, a shimmering apron of black silk, frilled up on to the shadowy white of the beach, languorously oblivious to the din going on in the town.

Brent drove up the hill alongside the curve of the beach. The narrow *calle* which the Azalea hotel backed on to was crowded with cars, and they had to drive along for quite a way before space could be found to park.

There were few lights along this way, for all the gaiety was directed towards the front where lighted balconies and forecourts were reflected in the deeper waters of the cove. But there were gardens here; great tumbling hedges of bougainvillea, hibiscus and sweet-smelling jasmine, whose perfume tugged at Faye's heart and brought tears of unhappiness to her eyes as she walked beside Brent.

Without warning a noisy group from one of the other hotels came rushing along the narrow street making for town. They pushed and crowded roughly by, and Brent caught Faye close to him and walked with a protective arm around her waist.

They moved together in the silence which descended once the group had dispersed. Faye's throbbing senses were tuned to her surroundings, to the strip of black sky above them hung with diamond-bright stars, to the muted sigh of the waves on the shore beyond the gardens, the perfume-laden breeze wafting in from the sea.

There was magic here, she could feel it. Something which, given the chance, could pluck at the heart-strings and stir one to the depths of one's soul. But it was not for her. The tense grip of Brent's arm around her waist told her that.

They stopped at a lighted gateway, and Faye lifted her head and braced herself for the evening to come. They had arrived at the Azalea Hotel and the Conde was waiting for her inside.

As though he read her thoughts Brent dropped his arm abruptly to his side. Though he guided her suavely indoors, the touch of his fingers on her arm was almost bruising. She sensed rather than saw the bitter gleam in his eyes.

As they moved into the party atmosphere inside the

hotel, no one would have suspected the undercurrent of feeling which stormed between them—no one except perhaps Greta.

Stunning in an oyster trouser-suit, smoke-grey pearls clipped in her ears, she enfolded Faye in a welcome. They dropped a kiss affectionately on each other's cheek, Spanish-style, while Brent removed Faye's wrap from her shoulders and handed it in at the cloakroom desk. Greta was quick to note Brent's taut look, the unhappy brightness in Faye's eyes.

Brightly she led them through into the dance area, where the small select clientele were enjoying the festivities laid on. She showed them to the bar and invited them to a drink, which they both declined; aware that, though outwardly smiling, they were as prickly as a couple of hedgehogs.

Bart came to join them, superbly dressed in a grey sharkskin suit, pearl-buttoned shirt and bow tie, but tonight he was obviously a busy man, and after chatting pleasantly for a while, both he and Greta were called away to attend to pressing matters to do with the hotel.

Faye wished she could have hurried away too. But it was pointless trying to run away from all that was inside her, that which would chain her for ever to the man standing close to her now.

Heavy-hearted, she let her gaze wander over the crowd. It was Brent who spotted the Conde first across the tastefully-lit interior. His voice was vibrant and mocking as he drew Faye's attention to the other man. 'Well, well! The old boy's really pulled out all the stops tonight. He looks like the star of an old Hollywood movie.'

Faye could see Enrique now. He did truly look striking in a shabby, debonair kind of way. His white dinner-jacket was an excellent fit, if a little threadbare at the elbows, and his black evening trousers made him look taller than ever, despite the fact that they appeared to be fraying a little around the ankles.

Faye had always been one to champion the under-dog. Annoyed at Brent's derisive tones she sprang to Enrique's defence, tossing her head as she retorted, 'Well, I think he looks rather sweet.'

She had no time to give much thought to the look of biting satire which Brent gave her, for the Conde had seen her and was rapidly making his way over. By the time he had reached her side Brent had disappeared.

'*Querida*, you look enchanting.' The Conde smiled down on her. She noticed that he had only been able to slip away because Carmina, her usual lacquered self in black tight-fitting frilled dress and brilliantly em-broidered black-fringed shawl, was engrossed with a couple with similar aquiline, olive-skinned features, and blazing black eyes, who Faye learned later were the flamenco dancers booked for the hotel cabaret spot.

But she cared little at the moment for the occupa-tion of others. Enrique was smiling at her. His soft dark eyes held no searing animosity as Brent's did; they were filled with disarming candour and benevolence and with his long dark hair and moustache giving him a cavalier look, he seemed to her the most restful person in the world to be with. When he drew her into his arms and guided her on to the dance floor she offered no word of protest.

Throughout the evening the Conde kept Faye almost exclusively to himself, and she was content to ease her aching heart in his arms. There were times when they didn't dance, of course; when Greta and Bart joined them, and with Carmina and Brent they sat at a table and ate tasty canapés, or laughed their way through jugs of Sangria, a heady mixture of red wine and brandy, crushed lemon and oranges.

Carmina, mellowed by the drink, lapsed sentimental on the Conde's shoulder and Greta worked hard to draw Brent and Faye together with her humour. But close to that muscular shoulder Faye could only show her appreciation with a brittle sparkle and Brent, tautly smiling, spent most of his time chatting to Bart.

After the cabaret act it was a relief, Faye found, to lose herself once more on the dance floor, in Enrique's arms. She did dance with Bart once, but he was enjoying himself in a working capacity and had to keep hurrying away to attend to hotel business. And Enrique was always close at hand. Drifting round in his arms, Faye might have been lulled into a state bordering on contentment but for the fact that the sight of Brent dancing every dance harped on her nerves.

His partners were invariably the stunningly attractive type with tanned bare backs and elaborately coiled hairdo's, and every one succumbed to his rugged charm before they were half way round the dance floor.

Occasionally Faye caught the blue glitter of his gaze while battling to appear unaffected at that which stirred in her the most primitive of all emotions, a gnawing, heart-twisting jealousy she had never thought herself capable of. She knew he was demonstrating for her benefit the devastating effect of his masculine personality on the opposite sex.

Naturally, when he finally came to ask her for a dance she moved woodenly in his arms. To all outward appearances she was just another partner in his arms. Only Faye knew that his white smile was contorted with some inner feeling known only to himself, that the biting satire was still very much in evidence in his blue eyes when he looked at her.

Throughout the dance he was aggressively courteous, and sneeringly charming; to such a degree that Faye would have walked off the dance floor more than once but for his firm hold on her. His reply to her ice-cold attitude was to clamp her against him in a steel-like embrace and whirl her around the room with a savage enjoyment which left her bruised and breathless.

Never had she been more glad to see the end of a dance, to hear the pianist and percussion group on the small dais bring the tune to a climactic finish. Trembling and close to tears, she didn't care that Brent swung roughly away from her. She had had enough of his acrimonious company for one evening.

When the music struck up again she found solace in Enrique's arms, and later when he guided her out on to a small open patio, leaving the music behind, she moved alongside him without a word.

She was raw and throbbing after the treatment she had received in Brent's arms, and wanted only the cool peace of the dark outdoors. They were in a tiny terraced section overlooking the cliff side garden, spiky with cactus and tropical shrubs. The starlit sky through the black tracery of the pines, the soft sigh from the black swell beyond the sea wall acted like a tonic on her ragged nerves.

She began to feel a calmness settling over her, an appreciation for the beauty of the night. And Enrique's arm around her was a comfort. He had been wooing her all evening with his soft Spanish words of endearment and his wickedly teasing manner. She knew he thought that he was the cause of her sentimental mood now, and that he meant to take advantage of it, and strangely enough she didn't care.

In a mood for retaliation where Brent was concerned she wondered if it might be possible to forget him in the Conde's embrace, to erase from her mind the rapturous memory of his lovemaking.

When Enrique drew her into his arms, breathing, 'Amor mio!' she offered no resistance.

Experimentally she waited for his lips to touch hers, but when they did she was in no way prepared for the flame of passion which she seemed to ignite in him.

Enrique's demanding mouth explored hers with a subtlety, an expertise which drained the life from her limbs. Never before had she known such an onslaught on her emotions. His worldliness, his experience with women was all there in his caress. She became putty in his arms and was sinking ... sinking beneath the overwhelming force of his magnetism, when a muttered oath from the doorway jerked her to her senses and quickly she moved out of the Conde's embrace.

It was Carmina's shadowy shape that she saw framed in the lighted doorway. Faye had been vaguely aware of the Andalusian woman's presence during the evening, in the companionship of the flamenco couple, or seated at the Templetons' table. The last time she had seen her she had been dancing with Bart. But she wasn't dancing now.

Faye was shocked at her changed look. Those aquiline features were drawn tight over the bone-structure of her face so that she resembled a raven-haired vulture framed in the doorway. But her eyes were the most frightening of all. Black as glistening jet, mirroring the night, they blazed with a murderous light that was almost inhuman in its intensity.

Faye stood rooted, impaled beneath the molten hate in that gaze; as the woman advanced on her she felt a faintness engulf her. Then into the doorway stepped Brent. His voice, carefully controlled, made a mockery of the scene as he said lazily, 'I haven't had a dance with you yet, Carmina. How about giving me that pleasure now?'

The Andalusian woman paused momentarily in her vicious advance on Faye and rapidly taking his cue, Brent gripped her arm and said gently, 'Let's go.'

As they turned back indoors Faye knew that he had seen as much as Carmina, for his features were set in granite and the glance he gave her held a hard, metallic light.

The Conde, apparently oblivious to the seething undercurrent of feeling, casually lit up a cigarette.

Trembling a little, Faye said, 'I think I'd better go in, Enrique.'

'But of course, *carina*.' All suave, dark-eyed innocence, the Conde took her arm and guided her back on to the dance floor.

Now Faye was equally ill at ease with the Conde. Her nerves stretched after his tempestuous embrace, she waited for the tune to finish, then smilingly broke away. Standing on the edge of the crowd she had no idea what she intended to do next, but her mind was made up for her in the form of a steely grip on her wrist.

Brent told her, 'Get your wrap, we're leaving.'

'I beg your pardon!' Glowering, Faye tried to remove herself from his grip, all the pain he had caused her during the evening culminating in white-hot anger. 'You are not, as far as I know, my keeper.'

For reply Brent jerked her across to the cloakroom desk. He threw her lace stole around her shoulders, and with an arm round her waist guided her roughly towards the outdoors.

On the way out they passed Greta. Brent said grimly as they went by, 'Goodnight, Greta. We've had a great time.'

'Goodnight, you two.' Greta watched Faye's forceful removal with wide-eyed wonder, a puzzled but not altogether unhappy light in her eyes.

Outside in the darkness Faye felt the cool air fanning her hot cheeks. She would have stood where she was, but Brent was in no mood for opposition, and yanked her out of the gate and along the narrow *calle* towards the car. Lips clenched, she thought of all the things she would tell him when she got her breath back.

At the car he opened the door and dumped her on the seat inside. Too spent to do anything but breathe furiously, Faye sat there as they took the road which curved down past the beach and then swung inland, aiming for the dark-shrouded countryside.

Once her anger had simmered down Faye was left with nothing but an abject misery. What a fool she had been to think she could forget Brent in another man's arms! Far from pouring abuse on him as she had planned to, she sat hunched in her seat watching dully as the black shapes of trees and villages flashed by.

Brent drove with the speed of a man who has had as much as he can take for one evening, and they arrived back at the *finca* in double quick time.

His headlights on, Brent, wearing a look of menacing calm, turned into the courtyard. Hardly waiting for the car to stop, Faye stepped out and hurried towards the farmhouse. She had got inside the dimly-lit door-way and was moving towards the communal kitchen when Brent caught her up and his fingers wrenching her shoulder he swung her round to face him. 'Oh no, you don't!' His white smile was a study in controlled wrath. 'This time you don't just disappear indoors. Not until we've had this thing out.'

Her own anger flaring again, Faye threw up her head, her tawny eyes flashing. 'What makes you think I want to discuss anything with you?'

'You don't have to tell me it's the Conde you want,' Brent sneered, 'but you're so busy flinging yourself into his arms that you've overlooked one thing. Carmina is a pretty explosive piece of merchandise. What are you going to do about her?'

'I can take care of myself.' Faye lifted her chin.

'Can you?' The sneer did not quite reach his eyes now as he flicked his questioning gaze over her pale features; over her bare slender shoulders beneath her lace wrap. 'I wonder? Carmina's out for your blood, and you know it.'

Faye wrenched herself from his grip, her shawl fall-ing from her shoulders as she did so. 'Oh? Who told you that?' she quivered, facing him. 'I suppose you've been talking to Señor Moreno.'

She had found out from Ana that Brent made monthly visits to her grandmother's lawyer for the purposes of paying his rent, and she knew that the two men were hand in glove with each other.

Brent looked slightly taken aback by her accusation. 'Don José Andrés might be a friend of mine,' he drawled, 'but he doesn't discuss his clients' affairs with me.'

'No?' It was Faye's turn to sneer. 'Then how is it you've known from the start that unless I happen to marry a Spaniard I don't inherit San Mateo?'

Brent shrugged, losing none of his disdain. 'As we were both about to take up residence under the same roof, José Andrés considered it prudent to familiarise me with the conditions of your stay.'

And if he hadn't, Faye mused to herself bitterly, *Brent wouldn't be thinking what he did of her now.*

She said through a blaze of tears at the thought, 'It seems to me it will be a good thing when your tenancy is up at San Mateo.'

'Don't worry,' Brent lashed back at her. 'I'm well ahead of schedule with my work on the course, and if I can get away before time, I will.'

'Well, that day can't come too soon for me!'

'Naturally,' Brent ripped through a tight-lipped smile. 'We all know what *your* plans are for the future.'

The strength drained from her at his potent remark. She parried, trying to sound cold, 'Do you have to shout? You'll wake up the Rodriguez couple.'

'To hell with the Rodriguez'.'

As she would have turned away Brent caught her wrist and jerked her towards him.

That savage smile still stamped on his face, his blue eyes dark and flame-lit as they bore into hers, he drawled, 'Sure, the Conde can give you San Mateo. But will that always be enough for you?'

Locked against him, his lips brushing perilously

close to hers, Faye fought hard to hold back the tears. How well he knew the power of his love, and how near she came to despising him for demonstrating that of which he was so sure.

Fighting the rising ecstasy in her, she said wearily, 'Brent, please let me go. I'm tired and I want to go to my room.'

'Just as you say.' His smiling features like a chalk mask, Brent dropped his arms and swung away towards the outdoors.

Faye didn't see him go, for through a curtain of tears she had already stumbled away to the darkness of her room. Inside, behind the door, she choked back the sobs that racked her.

If only she hadn't gone chasing after the Conde in the first place, she reproached herself. If only she hadn't wanted to prove to herself that Brent cared for her a little!

She had proved it all right. The memory of his kisses was still burned on her heart. But where had it got them?

She felt torn apart by her love for him. And Brent was convinced that her only interest was in snaring the Conde and thereby acquiring the wealth of San Mateo.

CHAPTER TEN

July came, bringing with it no changes at the *finca*, despite Faye's row with Brent and the explosive happenings on the night of the dance.

The Conde, convinced that he had in some way broken down Faye's defences with his kiss, called more frequently than ever under cover of good, neighbourly relationships. Carmina, as distrustful as a slant-eyed cat, watched everything that moved from under her smouldering lashes, and accompanied him on every visit.

About a fortnight after the dance the Templetons dropped in at the *finca*. The couple were in high spirits because the season was well under way, and with a good management staff they would now have more free time on their hands.

Their visit was a surprise in more ways than one, for out of the car the couple brought a set of gaily painted metal chairs, a matching table and a gay umbrella which slotted down a hole in the middle.

Faye demurred at this extravagance, but in her kindly way Greta said with wide-eyed diplomacy, 'Darling, we've been wanting to get rid of this lot for ages! We never know what to do with discarded stuff around the hotel.'

And just to make it even more all right Bart grinned, struggling to look apologetic, 'We hope you don't mind us lumbering you with them, Faye?'

It was agreed that the outdoor furniture might have been made for the strip of grassy terrace along the south wall of the *finca*. There one could sit in comparative shade and contemplate the sweep of valley shimmering in the July heat. Ana brought out a jug of freshly made lemon juice plus a dish of ice cubes, and everyone sat quenching their thirst and languishing in the sultry warmth.

The Templetons popped in on one or two afternoons a week after that. Brent was always around. Ana had said that it was too hot now for him to work on the golf course in the afternoons, and Faye digested this information warily. She had a feeling that he stayed around the *finca* purposely to keep his eye on the social scene.

For herself Faye found these gatherings wearing on the nerves. She felt suffocated by the presence of the others; Greta watching her with puzzled concern and speculating, Faye knew, on her washed out look and shadowed eyes; Carmina, ever on the alert, viewing her in a different way with eyes like blazing black coals beneath her sultry lashes, Brent tense and smiling, giving nothing away in his lazy conversation.

Bart, with his mature humour and carefree manner, was the only one with whom Faye could feel relaxed. And then of course there was the Conde, who was so blissfully detached from what was noticeable in all but the Templetons that Faye automatically turned to him for release from the strain.

She knew that when she wandered to the edge of the terrace and Enrique, by her side, pointed out to her an exotic bird winging its way up the valley or some well-known peak in the range of heat-veiled mountains, Carmina, though giving the appearance of being pleasantly engaged in conversation at the table, watched through her black lashes: but rather than subject herself to the atmosphere around the table, Faye chose to linger in the Conde's company.

After all, she told herself, they were simply admiring the view. What harm was there in that? If only she had known the havoc she was creating for herself with these innocent gestures.

One afternoon in particular remained for ever imprinted on her memory.

On this occasion she had spent most of her time with Enrique. He had been giving her some ideas on how to brighten up the strip of terrace with a few flower pots, and towards the end of the afternoon, just before the Templetons were leaving, he had playfully pointed out that he had pots galore at his house, and as she hadn't visited him for a few weeks, it was high time she came over to pick up a few.

Of course he didn't offer to drive her over himself with Carmina breathing down their necks. Indeed his manner, whenever they were in the company of the others, was always slyly modulated to that of the gallant friend with accommodating good humour, and nothing more.

Laughingly Faye told him she would drive over immediately they had left, and she noticed that Carmina made a point of going to wave the Templetons off at the lane entrance. When she and Brent and the Conde had drifted into the courtyard, the Andalusian woman was waiting, with a small smile curling her red lips, at the wheel of the Conde's car.

Enrique climbed in and gave Faye a wave. '*Hasta luego*,' he saluted with that naughty twinkle which was meant for her eyes only. Faye watched him take his seat in the open-topped car, his long hair swirling and his black eyes flashing devilment despite his effort to appear the phlegmatic nobleman.

Once they had swerved away down the track Faye began to think about making for her own car. Brent was beside her and she sensed the steely antagonism in the set of his muscular shoulders beneath his vivid blue shirt, in the twist of his smile, clamped over bitter humour.

Too spent to think of arguing, Faye hung about, wishing there was something she could say to break the deadlock between them. At last Brent broke it for her, but in a way which only added fuel to the damped-down blaze which raged between them.

With sneering contempt in his tones, he drawled, watching her, 'You should have a nice cosy time over there in the Conde's pad—under the pretext of gathering flower pots, of course.'

Faye replied with acid smoothness, 'If you're worried about what goes on behind closed doors, why don't you come and join us?'

'Not me!' Brent's laugh was hard and metallic. 'I've got work to do, remember?'

Faye was all too aware what he meant by that. He might be taking things quietly in the afternoons, but she knew that he was putting in long hours at the Zarzamora course in the evenings, until dark most nights, so that he could complete his contract ahead of schedule. *Just to get away from the* finca.

The hurt made tears rush to her eyes. Her tones high-pitched and trembling, she managed to thrust back behind a veneer of brittle unconcern, 'Of course I forgot! You can't wait to get the golf course finished so that you can say farewell to Majorca ... and as the sun sinks slowly in the west and all that....' she mimicked with a smile, but she felt as though her heart would break.

She had to lower her gaze quickly, afraid that Brent would see all that was written there.

'That's right,' he agreed, watching her. 'Once the last green is completed there's not a thing that can keep me here.'

'Well, put in a few squares of turf for me, while you're at it,' she flashed at him shakily, then swung away to her car.

It occurred to her that there was something odd about the steering the moment she started out. But her heart and mind were full of the torment that Brent could inflict with his words and she wanted only to remove herself rapidly from his presence.

A little blindly, as he too swung away towards the house, she shot across the courtyard towards the winding cart track. The moment she curved away to take the tortuous route down she knew there was something wrong with her brakes.

Normally she kept her foot half on the pedal on this twisting descent, but now the thing flapped useless under her foot and her wheels were gathering momentum at an alarming speed.

The banked-up earth of the hillside flanking the

track flashed by her windows. On a bend it reared up, coming for her windscreen, and spun away the hairsbreath of a second before contact as she battled with the crazy steering wheel.

Shock paralysed her. Every vestige of colour drained from her face as she careered at suicidal speed down the rocky route, and she realised there was nothing between her and the tree-lined lane in the valley below except the jutting bluffs of the hillside ... and possibly oblivion.

Her tyres burned up in the blazing dust. Into the mad nightmare of trying to stay alive the odour of singeing rubber came to assail her nostrils; stones and rocks flew from her path. Tree stumps, low walls and mounds of solid rock hurled themselves at her until she was a sobbing wreck and on the point of giving up.

Her arms ached from the effort of trying to remain in control. Her brain was a whirl, numbed in this lonely, terrifying world of unhampered speed. She thought she would never reach the floor of the valley in one piece, but suddenly, after what seemed a hundred years of fighting at the wheel, the level ground came beneath her tyres.

Still she couldn't relax. If anything the danger was greater than ever now. The lane was narrow and flanked by every conceivable obstacle, and she had no way of reducing the momentum with which the car had come hurtling down the cart track.

Now that the shock had subsided, hysteria rose in her throat. She would never do it, she told herself. Never be able to avoid hitting something before she stopped! Collision was staring her in the face and she felt helpless to prevent it.

The car bucked and leapt in her hands as the trunks of the trees rushed by. Ahead was the sheep shed, then the gatepost of their paddock came looming into view; Faye saw it rushing towards her windscreen and then blackness.

She didn't know it then, but Ana and Anofre and a couple of farm labourers had been watering tomatoes on the strip beside the sheep shed. They had seen her crashing, stampeding, dust-clouded descent from the courtyard, and came running across the field to the scene of the disaster.

But they were not as fast as Brent, who sprinted down the cart track and arrived ahead of them.

His was the first face that Faye saw when she opened her eyes. It was ashen-looking, and working in a strange way. His clouded blue eyes raked hers, and when he saw that she had come to no great harm he gave vent to his feelings explosively, and with white-hot anger.

'This heap of metal belongs in the junk yard!' He raked her car with his gaze. 'It's a wreck, and you're lucky it hasn't caused you trouble before this. Do you realise you might have been killed?'

'I'm all right.' Sitting up, Faye wanted to reassure herself as well as Brent on this point. She had received a slight bump on the forehead through being thrown against the windscreen, but her safety belt had saved her from anything worse. Her father had drilled it into her to always fasten the seat belt around her even if she was only going to post a letter, and she was glad now that she had obeyed his rigid instructions.

Releasing her, Brent picked her up in his arms. 'I'm all right,' Faye reiterated weakly. But he carried her every step of the way back up the cart track, and Ana ran alongside ready to precede him through the farm-house to Faye's room.

He laid her gently on the bed. Under his stringent gaze she said brightly, fighting off the wave of dizziness which threatened to engulf her, 'I'll just lie here for a while, then I'll be fine.'

Brent looked convinced when she smiled and forced a sigh of relaxation from her lips. As she closed her eyes she heard him go out, and later his car started up in the courtyard, and she knew he was on his way to the golf course.

Ana had gone to fetch a rag soaked in some local herb remedy to reduce the swelling on her forehead, and as she lay there alone Faye relived her nightmare drive down the twisting cart track. Strong in her mind also was the picture of Carmina, waiting poised at the top of the track in the Conde's car with that funny little smile on her face.

Only Faye knew how closely the Andalusian woman had watched her during the afternoon in Enrique's company. And she had gone, ostensibly to wave off the Templetons, while Brent and the Conde were engaged in a last-minute chat. That had given her several moments alone in the courtyard. Had it been long enough for her to tamper with Faye's car? Carmina was no stranger to the inside workings of an engine, as she had shown in her deft handling of the Conde's car. And over in the lean-to shed she would have been well hidden from view.

Faye shuddered at the thought. But perhaps she was letting her imagination run away with her. The car was old, as Brent had said, and just lately she had been unable to find the money to have it serviced. It wasn't impossible that something had given when she raced out of the lean-to shed and across the courtyard, and once she was on the slope of the track it had been too late to investigate the trouble.

This latter theory seemed the most likely explanation. And yet ... try as she would, Faye couldn't rid herself of the picture of the smouldering-eyed Carmina sitting at the wheel of the Conde's car with that feline smile curling her lips.

Ana returned with the soaked head dressing. Before she left to return to her work in the tomato field Faye scribbled a note to the Conde, to be delivered by the farm-hand who lived in the same hamlet and who would shortly be finishing work.

She didn't say anything about her mishap. She wrote simply that something else had turned up and that she would have to postpone her visit until another time.

Alone in the house, she dozed until dusk. It was the clatter of Ana working in the cookhouse which stirred her. Rising, she realised she would have to prepare herself a scratch meal.

What an effort it was to lift her head from the pillow! Thank goodness once she was on her feet a little of the fogginess left her.

She walked carefully and erect out of doors, knowing that Anofre, herding a pair of calves up from the fields, and Ana in the cookhouse, watched her with penetrating anxiety. Everything was fine as she walked across the courtyard, then just as she was making for the cookhouse doorway her legs buckled beneath her. She would have crumpled like a rag doll but for Anofre's presence of mind, and Ana rushed out pan in hand to grab her arm on the other side. '*Dios mio!*' the woman exclaimed darkly. 'You should be in bed.'

Faye laughed shakily as she sank down on a pile of empty vegetable crates. 'It's nothing. I just got up a little too quickly, that's all. Once I've had a cup of tea I shall be back to my old self.'

Ana and Anofre looked doubtful, but as she thanked them for their assistance and proceeded towards the cookhouse there was nothing they could do except carry on, a little helplessly, with their own chores. Faye knew that her face must be ghostly white from the way she felt, but she was determined to shake off the giddiness at all costs.

She had prepared her tea and was endeavouring with trembling hands to pick up the cup, when car headlights swung into the courtyard. Brent was back earlier than usual. She knew who it was by the sound of his rapid footsteps on the rough surface outside the house.

In the cookhouse she kept her back turned towards the doorway, but she knew that Ana and Anofre had intercepted him outside and that they were having a whispered consultation in the farmhouse doorway. A few seconds later Brent came striding over to the cookhouse. He had a light jacket which he sometimes wore in the evenings over his arm, and dropping it around Faye's shoulders he said briskly, 'Put this on. We're going out.'

Faye swung on him and lifted her startled gaze, feverishly bright in her white face, to ask, 'Where to?'

'To the clinic in Llosaya.'

Faye shrank back. She had no money to meet medical bills. In a panic she stammered, 'But I'm perfectly all right. I don't want to go to the clinic.'

'We're going just the same.' Brent took her arm.

Faye had no choice but to let him guide her towards his car. Tears of weakness were in her eyes as she took her seat, wondering if she would ever find a way out of the mess she was in. Her car was wrecked at the bottom of the hill, and added to this she could be saddled with a bill for doctors' fees. And she hadn't sold a picture in weeks. Not one. She had driven down to the showrooms hopefully most days, ignoring the extra cost in petrol, but the awful truth was that no one wanted her pictures.

But she felt too wretched now to care either way. Her head was throbing and she was having a hard time fighting back the tears as she sat and watched the fields and hedges flash by, as Brent drove rapidly towards Llosaya.

In the clinic all was cool efficiency. Faye went through every known test, to hear with relief, at the end, that she was suffering from no more than a mild concussion, and that a good night's sleep plus a couple of days' resting up was all she needed to make a complete recovery.

She went out to meet Brent feeling easier in one way, but troubled in another. The check-up had been thorough, and she dreaded to think what the cost was going to be to her pocket. Nervously she waited as the doctor shook hands with Brent, but no mention was made of money. She presumed worriedly that the bill would come later.

It was late when they got back to the *finca*. With that mask of impregnability back in place, Brent asked her if she would be all right as he left her at the door of the farmhouse. Faye nodded, and thanked him in the same aloof way for his assistance, then went straight to her room.

Luckily she experienced no more after-effects from the accident. The bruise on her forehead disappeared overnight, and by the next day she was going about her business as usual around the farmhouse. But the car incident had brought to a head all her anxieties concerning the disastrous state of her financial affairs, and the gnawing worry of her empty purse filled her days.

Though she tried hard to hide all the signs of her impecunious state it was difficult to keep face, especially when Brent was around. She wanted to crawl into a hole with embarrassment one morning when he stopped her in the courtyard. She had seen Anofre having a few whispered words with him and had hoped fervently that it had nothing to do with her. Then Brent had come over. 'They want to know when you're going to do something about having your car removed. Apparently it's blocking the paddock entrance, and the shepherd's having the devil of a job getting the sheep around it.'

'Oh!' For a moment Faye's face was stained with colour. Then, battling to sound off-hand, she said, 'Of course! I'll get someone from my garage in Llosaya to come and tow it away. Naturally I meant to have it fixed ... it's just that ... I never got round to it.'

She was glad when Brent nodded and continued towards his car. She knew he had noticed her reluctance to go with him to the clinic, and she thought he had eyed her blushing embarrassment rather sharply.

As soon as he had gone she walked to Caliséta and rang up the garage. Heaven knew how she was going to pay the bill, but she dared not back down from her showy promise.

The fact that her stock of provisions had finally come to an end was also causing her considerable concern. Oh, there was plenty of food at the farmhouse, but the meals Ana prepared for her husband and the farmhands were not the kind she could take to. In any case she had always a point of keeping house for herself, so at all costs she had to uphold this image.

She might have managed rather well at covering up her scant diet but for the fact that the evenings were hot and airless and everyone, Brent included, spent their time out of doors before turning in for the night. This made it a harassing task indeed working in the cookhouse. Through the day there was no one about to see her making do with a sandwich of bread and cheese, or some of the fruit left over from the market; but it was irritating to find that no matter how she timed her evening meal after the heat of the day, Brent was always somewhere around watching her every move.

One night she almost lost her temper when he strolled over to the cookhouse to lean in the lighted doorway while she was working. For the past weeks there had never been anything but friction between them, and it didn't help her now to know that his sardonic blue gaze followed her movements.

And of course he would have to comment on the

sparse layout of her tray.

'Who wants to eat on these hot nights?' she replied with brittle humour. 'The thought of food nauseates me. And I'm not terribly enamoured either,' she gave him a withering look, 'of someone hovering at my shoulder when I'm cooking.'

Brent flicked a look towards the hearth and said drily, 'Do you always get temperamental when you're boiling an egg?'

'You should see me when I'm cooking a roast, or basting a chicken,' Faye quipped tartly.

With slightly trembling hands she fumbled to drop the egg in the egg cup, then swinging up the tray she swept towards the door. He didn't move as she made for the outside so that she was compelled to brush close against him to get by. She held the tray between clenched fists, hindered by his indolent bulk, and but for the fact that she was perilously close to tears of defeat she would have tossed the whole thing in his lap.

CHAPTER ELEVEN

GRETA said it was too hot to hang around the *finca*. Always the life and soul of the party, she pointed out that there was much more fun to be had at Porto Cristo, where one could splash about in the sea or the hotel pool to keep cool.

It was Brent whom she teased into accepting the idea, but Faye knew she was included in the invitation along with the Conde and Carmina. The Andalusian woman had behaved in her usual lacquered, auto-cratic way when calling again at the *finca*. Faye's car had been removed by that time, and if Carmina knew anything about the faulty brakes she had given noth-ing away in her sphinxlike expression.

Greta put up with the Spanish woman's chilly presence because she liked to lark about with the Conde, but although she too was somewhat impaled by Enrique's charm, he was to her just someone whom Faye was a little sweet on.

Two or three afternoons a week the party met at the Templetons' hotel in Porto Cristo. Brent had made a habit of driving Faye over when starting out himself after a morning's work at the golf course and the Conde and Carmina were usually there when they arrived.

To Faye these summer afternoons were the most bitter-sweet she had known. She had Brent to herself on the drive to Porto Cristo and though their conversation consisted of no more than polite exchanges, it was a crumb of comfort to have him there at her side.

In the hotel pool, too, he was never far away from her. Carmina preferred to sit with a herb liqueur at a table under the pine trees, and the Conde had a hard time of it matching Brent's speed in the water.

In the gay holiday atmosphere, the hotel crowded with guests and the cove and beach a riot of colour and sound, Faye might have been tempted to join in the fun; but her financial worries were dogging her. She wondered how much longer she could keep going at the *finca* without funds.

Of course she did her best to hide her anxieties. She tossed a ball about to Enrique in the pool, and made trips to the beach to swim in the cove along with the others, but her tawny eyes were dark and troubled and she was fast becoming a shadow of herself through eating too little.

It was Greta who noticed her peaked look. One afternoon when Bart was politely showing Carmina the Continental decor of the dining room, and Brent and Enrique were in the pool, she asked casually as they lounged together at one of the hotel tables, 'How are the pictures going? Sold any yet?'

'Nope, not one!' Faye battled to sound nonchalant, but knowing it was useless with Greta's perceptive blue gleam on her. She slumped and said with a wry smile, 'I've a feeling this is something else you could have told me that first night on the boat.'

Greta nodded. 'So many artists come to the island as hopefully as you did. Hundreds of them.'

'I've been finding that out for myself these past few weeks,' Faye agreed glumly. 'There must be a dozen paintings to every tourist in Llosaya showrooms alone.'

'Well, never mind. Cheer up, poppet!' Greta made an effort to snap her out of her despondency. 'Someone will come along and buy one of your nice pictures, I'm sure of it.'

Knowing that she was only being kind, Faye tried to smile.

In the silence Greta toyed with the idea of offering a little assistance, but she was all too aware of the proud light in Faye's amber gaze, the independent thrust of her small chin, and wisely refrained.

Just when Faye was trying to pull herself together after admitting her dreadful failure, Brent climbed out of the pool beside their table. Knowing that he too watched her like a hawk these days, she averted her over-bright gaze from his blue one and shakily mumbled something about going to cool off, then ran and took a dive into the pool.

She was glad the Conde was there to swing her into his arms once she had broken the surface. Splashing and laughing with him was the recreation she needed to forget, for a while, her crushing worries.

Of course this didn't please Carmina, who had returned to the table beside the pool and watched her embracing Enrique in the water, her black eyes molten fire beneath her lashes. But Faye was past caring about the Andalusian woman. Brent was talking to Greta at the table, and intent on keeping up a carefree pose whenever he looked her way, she encouraged Enrique all she could as they brawled about like children in the water.

Brent usually drove back to the golf course towards the cool of evening. He had to drop Faye of at the *finca* several miles further on before he could start work and she knew this must be a nuisance to him. But conversation was so stretched between them she never got round to offering to return home some other way, and Brent made no move either to suggest alternative arrangements.

Generally speaking Faye found the lack of personal transport a terrible handicap in the country. One day she took a bus down to Llosaya. The garage people had told her her car was ready and she had come down without an idea in her head as to how she was going to pay the bill; she must have known that Tomeu, the friendly blue-overalled mechanic she had dealt with ever since coming out to the island, would smilingly wave aside her stammering excuses. With true Majorcan disregard for time and official business he insisted, beaming generously, '*Es igual, es igual!*' Tomorrow, next week, what did it matter when she paid the bill?

Blessing all trusting Majorcans, Faye drove away, hardly able to believe her luck. She had only the petrol that was left in the tank, of course, but with economical use she was able to get out and about around the *finca* almost as well as before.

Then one wonderful August day it happened! Someone bought a picture. Well, not just one!

She hadn't been down to Llosaya since picking up the car, but one morning, praying that the petrol would eke out, she decided to make what would probably turn out to be another fruitless trip to the showrooms. And lo and behold! When she arrived at the renovated stables on the corner of a busy tourist thoroughfare, it was to learn that all three of the pictures she had deposited there had gone to a buyer several days before.

Faye couldn't believe her good fortune, but as the man in charge paid her he told her it usually happened like that. Someone would take a fancy to the work of a certain artist and buy the whole stock of their paintings.

Faye was in her seventh heaven. Oh, she saw now, she told herself gaily, where she had gone wrong. She had been frightening her chances away rushing down to town every day and enquiring wistfully about her pictures. The mishap with the car had put an end to her frenzied trips and once her impatience had been curbed it turned out that her pictures sold as well as anyone else's!

She revelled in the joy of buying a whole load of groceries, and drove back to San Mateo with a full petrol tank and her repair bill at the garage paid.

That evening she prepared a meal with relish in the cookhouse. She had no worries now about Brent hovering near while she worked. She was solvent again. She had done what she had come out to the island to do, make her living by her own efforts. She was proud of her success, and she let him see it in the flamboyant way she ladled out succulent asparagus tips on to her plate, the way she arranged the dish of fried scampi on her tray.

She noticed that there were no comments tonight. Brent just leaned in the doorway with his usual indolent curiosity. Well, she hoped he was taking note of the savoury display, the bottle of sparkling table wine. She would show him that she was capable of providing herself with more than a boiled egg!

Often after that Faye brushed past Brent with a well-stocked tray. She could afford to meet his blue gaze now with a look of showy independence. In the daytime too, at the hotel pool or down on the beach at Porto Cristo, she took pleasure in waving her new-found status as an artist under his nose. The laughter on her lips was real now as she splashed about uproariously with the Conde in the pool, and when they went to lounge around on the soft sand in the cove her swinging walk a little ahead of Brent was designed to convey her oozing success. It was true her heart ached beneath her lofty behaviour, but her paintings were selling well and more than anything she wanted Brent to know this.

She was supremely sure of herself around the *finca*; no need to creep about now. Whenever she ran into Brent her hazel-gold eyes flashed challengingly, and she would toss her flame locks in a gesture of airy confidence. And when the matter of the clinic bill came up she left him in no doubt as to the stability of her affairs.

They were setting off to the Hotel Azalea for a cooling swim on this scorching August afternoon. As always she and Brent had little to say to one another, but the mail had arrived. 'Ana told me to give you this,' Faye said, then withholding the crackly official-looking envelope with the bold blue print, 'It's from the clinic in Llosaya.'

'That's right,' Brent nodded as she examined it, 'it was my idea to have a doctor look at you, so I told them to send the bill to me.'

'But it was I who had the check-up,' Faye answered coolly, 'naturally I prefer to settle my own debts.'

'Just as you say,' Brent shrugged casually. 'It's only that medical fees tend to be pretty high over here, and I wouldn't want to land you in trouble with any steep charges incurred.'

'Open it, please.' Faye thrust the envelope at him. 'I shall pay the bill next time I go to Llosaya.'

She was more than a little staggered when she saw

the cost of the clinic's services, but she was careful not to let Brent see this. And what did it matter anyway? She was selling several pictures at a time now. Her income was more than enough to tide her over small setbacks like these.

She thrust the bill into her handbag with expressionless calm. 'As I said, I shall attend to it on my next trip to town.'

'If you prefer it that way.' Shrugging the matter off with the same casual air, Brent guided her towards his car.

Within minutes they were cruising along the country roads towards the coast. Faye sat erect and aloof in her seat as the cool air wafted in through the open windows; she could of course have driven her own little blue car now that it was running reasonably well again, but she preferred the acid-sweet torture of Brent's nearness to no Brent at all.

Likewise, though he knew she had her car back, Brent made no move to put an end to the assistance he had offered at the start.

The end of August brought a swarm of activity to the *finca*. The almond crop was ready for picking and groups of peasant women from the village, huge straw hats to protect them from the sun and voluminous skirts to combat the coarse grass, trudged in with bags and baskets.

Wiry old men beat at the nuts with long fishing-rod-like canes making them clatter down on to the green nets spread out below the trees and nimble-footed schoolboys with the agility of monkeys climbed to the uppermost branches to make sure that not one precious green nodule remained.

Up in the courtyard Anofre supervised a noisy clattering contraption which shelled the outer husks from the almond nuts and sacked them ready for the warehouse.

No sooner had the nut picking season finished than the grape season began. The women were carted across the fields in a tractor-drawn conveyance and deposited among the vines where they filled baskets taller than themselves with the fat juicy wine grapes. Middle-aged and grandmothers alike, they made the most of the scant male assistance available, flirting outrageously with the men as they carried the baskets to the tractor and receiving as a reward some succinct reply so that the valley echoed with the coarse peasant laughter and the ribald remarks.

In the balmy September days the clientele at the Hotel Azalea dwindled hardly at all. Majorca's golden autumn was preferred by many to the harsh, fretful heat of the summer, and the town and beaches of Porto Cristo continued to reverberate with sound.

Draped on the green lawn in the dappled shade of the pines at the hotel, the view of a blue sky softened now by fleecy clouds; of autumn flowers recovering from the stultifying heat and the sea scattered with coins of sunlight beyond the sea wall, was a restful one. Faye stared into space, hugging her knees, occasionally letting her glance trail over the others who lounged in chairs or on the grass around her.

Bart snoozed with a straw hat over his eyes, glad of a break after the rush of supervising the guests at the lunch tables. Greta was also resting her bones after some hard work around the hotel, but chattered no less animatedly to Brent, who sat hunched on the grass beside her chair. Faye let her glance rest for a moment on the tanned lean jaw that she had come to know so well, on the broad blue-clad shoulders and crisp, undisturbed brown hair. Soon now he would have no excuse to laze away his afternoons at the hotel. The killing heat of summer had passed, and he had work to do at the golf course.

Her lashes lowered momentarily as she battled with a shard of pain. Torturing though these weeks had been, so achingly close to Brent and yet a soured and embittered world apart, she didn't know what she was going to do when they came to an end.

Quickly she took her glance on to Carmina. Far too rigid in her ways to sit on the grass, the Andalusian woman was perched on the edge of a chair. In the heat of the day she had been accustomed to fanning herself briskly with a lace and flower-patterned fan, and the habit died hard, for she wafted herself furiously even though the air now was pleasantly breatheable.

Of course, Faye knew that this was because the Conde was lying close alongside her on the grass. Poor Carmina! In a way Faye could sympathise with her. She dragged herself out to the hotel two or three times a week, put up with the rude stares of foreigners, all to keep an eye on Enrique. And Enrique made the trip because he wanted San Mateo and marriage to Faye would give it to him. And Faye came because it was the only place where she could be near to Brent, apart from the *finca* where they frequently fought.

She lowered her gaze again over her wry amusement. They were all caught up in a ridiculous game of follow-my-leader and no one wanted to drop out; although she had a feeling that Enrique was growing impatient.

Never very serious, his wooing of her had been done with nothing more than calculated charm, a dash of Spanish gallantry here and there and a flair for poetic phrases. She doubted whether he could put himself out to be more than a lighthearted philanderer with any woman.

However, he did have a purpose, and on these last few outings he had stayed closer than ever to Faye. On the receiving end of his jaded wit, his expertise for putting into words all that a woman wants to hear, Faye had been breathless and smiling, but conscious only of Carmina's wildly fluttering fan. And it was on afternoons like this, when Enrique had been specially attentive towards her, that she knew Carmina eyed her from beneath her sweep of black lashes with volcanic hate.

Her fan flew now because Enrique was trailing a blade of grass playfully along Faye's bare arm. Faye went back to staring out to sea.

Later, when the blade of grass had grown limp in his hands, the Conde sat up. As though he had been giving it some thought he said, fixing Faye with his magnetic gleam, 'Now that it is cooler, we should go for a drive one afternoon.' Though they couldn't see the towering mountain range from this side of the island, Faye knew he had been musing on them when he added, 'What about a trip to Alaro?'

'What a splendid idea!' It was Greta's voice. Not as engrossed in her chat with Brent as she had appeared to be, she kicked her husband's propped-up chair from under him. 'We've always wanted to see Alaro, haven't we, Bart?'

'What's that? Oh yes ... delighted!' Shocked out of his doze, Bart came to with a dazed smile.

A little nonplussed at the enthusiasm displayed for a suggestion he had made purely with himself and Faye in mind, the Conde could only give a gracious smile.

Carmina, who seldom spoke a word, gushed darkly, 'The view from the Moorish stronghold is truly a wonderful sight. I'm sure we would all consider the trip worthwhile, Mrs. Templeton.'

Brent, who to Faye's mind watched Carmina closely these days, spoke easily, at the same time including himself in the invitation. 'I'm not sure the going will be all that smooth in that bomb you call a car, Enrique. If Faye goes with anyone, she goes with me.'

'But of course, my dear Brent.' Enrique, never one

to put up a fight, was only too eager now to have a jolly party. 'What does it matter! We'll all be together at the top.'

The outing was arranged for the following afternoon, and after lunch Faye dressed in slim-fitting slacks and a cool blouse, for Enrique had told her that the climb before they reached the top of the bluff was an arduous one. But though she recalled his words, it was Brent who occupied her thoughts as she put the finishing touches to her toilet.

She often wondered if he had deduced more from the circumstances surrounding her car mishap than he let her believe. He had taken care not to leave her alone with Carmina since that day.

She shrugged off the notion. What did it matter anyway? Brent had arranged it so that they would be travelling together, but not, she told her wildly leaping heart, because it gave him any particular pleasure. Just the same, strained though she would be by his nearness, she couldn't help but anticipate with madly racing pulses the sweetness his company offered.

Hiding it all behind the lofty air she had adopted since obtaining her new-found independence as a painter, she went out to the courtyard to find Brent was waiting for her beside his car. 'All set?' He watched her walk towards him, then nodded in the direction of the lane. 'The others are lined up keeping an ear cocked for the signal.'

Despite the gnawing misery mingling with the happy pain in her heart at the sight of him, Faye couldn't hold back a tiny spurt of laughter. 'Are they here already?' The sun was shining, and dragonflies hovered and darted in the golden light. Somehow she felt it was going to be a wonderful afternoon.

His eyes bluer than the delicious, cool blue of the sky behind him, Brent helped her into her seat.

When they were out in the lane he sounded his horn.

The Templetons in their smart red Renault gave a wave before pulling away, and leading the procession the Conde's vintage car set off with a thump and a bang.

Faye paid no further attention to the preceding vehicles. She wanted to soak up and treasure to the end these last moments alone with Brent, for something told her that their time together was running out.

These were memories that would have to serve her for a lifetime, for no other man could shake her world as Brent had done. And when he went from her....

She turned her tear-starred gaze out of the window at her side. Here she was getting maudlin, and she had promised herself she would make the best out of the short time left to her.

With an effort she gave herself to the view and a short while later she gasped at the lovely sight as a pair of birds, disturbed by the sound of the cars, rose up huge and long-beaked, their wings mottled and glistening in the sunlight. Brent told her their name in Mallorquene; he had learned a lot about the countryside during his working days at the golf course. As they branched off on to the road to the mountains he pointed out to her familiar trees and bushes, for despite her long association with the island she had never discovered their names.

In the village of Alaro women were doing the family washing in a great communal stone trough in a triangle of shade as the cars crunched by, taking the stony track uphill. Iron gates were opened at intervals along the way, welcoming visitors to the private grounds of the castle.

The route grew progressively steeper. The terrain was of undulating woods and greenery, later giving way to craggy rocks with weather-sculptured faces, and gnarled tree shapes. They passed a lovely white house on the roadside, the only one in the vast loneliness of the mountainside, and after that the route was no more than a tortuous, zig-zagging dust trail, wringing out a monotonous drone from the car engines as they continued up, climbing, climbing into the sky.

With anyone else Faye might have been nervous, for at intervals she caught glimpses of the vast sweep of plain flowing like a modest patchwork green river at the foot of the mountain slopes below her. And a few inches space at the roadside was all the separated the car wheels from bottomless, tree-tangled valleys. But Brent's brown hands were steady on the wheel and the easy, relaxed way with which he manoeuvred the car somehow communicated itself to her.

The Conde's vintage contraption was doing marvels. Though it snorted and sighed like an overworked mule, it kept up the pace ahead of the Templetons' Renault. Faye could see Greta's fair head swivelling this way and that through the rear window, and she could just imagine the older woman chortling and gasping with excitement as they hung suspended over the views.

Almost as high as the clouds, they came at last to the end of the road as far as the cars were concerned. In a shallow depression there was parking space and a truly rustic Majorcan café, its walls of rough bamboo canes strung together. One could sit inside at one of the knobbly trestle tables or outdoors at a big communal circular table.

In another open-air section there was a tremendous fireplace area where the proprietor told them huge logs blazed in the winter for visitors willing to brave the keen winds at this height for a glimpse of the castle. Greta was fascinated, and wanted to peep into everything.

Drinks were taken after the gruelling drive. Carmina was at home among her own kind and enjoyed a chat, in her stilted, unbending way, with the proprietor's wife, a mainlander. They were told that the object of their visit was a steady half hour's climb away, and when everyone was rested they started out.

Faye would dearly have loved to walk hand in hand with Brent up here in the crisp, sparkling air, but she knew no way to bridge the gulf that separated them. So, with a smile on her lips, because it was impossible not to be intoxicated by the beauty of their surroundings, she set forth along the ribbon of path which snaked up the mountain slope towards the summit.

Greta was a willing second, followed by her husband's stalwart figure, and Brent conversed lazily with the Conde at the rear, assisting Carmina here and there as the path grew steeper.

Faye walked with a spring in her step. Up here suspended above the world, she felt refreshingly free for a time from all the earthly afflictions of the mind—and the heart. Greta, in her white trouser suit and brilliant patterned blouse, puffed and stumbled in her wake, begging laughingly, 'Hold on, pet! You're making us all feel our age.'

'I second that,' Bart grumbled goodnaturedly, steadying his wife by the arm when she became over-ambitious up the rocky route, and mopping his brow at intervals with his spotless white handkerchief.

Faye tossed a smile down to them now and then. She had never given much thought to the fact that she was so much younger than the rest of them. There had been times during these past weeks when she had felt as old as Methuselah; so much so that it was a unique experience now to give vent to her youthful vigour.

She had tied her hair into a girlish ponytail for freedom of movement and she knew that Brent's blue eyes rested on her for most of the time as, with the mountain air whipping colour into her cheeks, she moved energetically up the pebbly path. She had an idea that he could have outpaced her had he so wished, but he seemed to prefer to stay at the rear, a little behind the Conde and close to Carmina.

The winding path led them across the last hump of the mountain, and from here they took the looping route which hugged the perpendicular wall of the towering bluff. Faye felt the excitement coursing through her veins as she caught glimpses of the crumbling Moorish stronghold which littered the crown of the bluff.

Every now and again they came to a colourful religious tile set in the face of the rock. The men were interested in the dynamite holes still visible where the engineers had blasted to construct this modern route for visitors. Strange birds flapped out from dark hiding places, and clumps of brightly coloured weeds clung stubbornly to the infertile wall of towering granite.

At last Faye came to the stone gateway of the Moorish keep. She was well ahead of the others and had plenty of time to examine the square cavities in the walls inside the gateway, originally for lanterns, and the slit-like openings in the battlement walls which gave one a restricted view of the rock face of the cliff that plummeted out of sight below among the sparse greenery.

Viewing the typical Moorish archway inside the entrance and the crumbling ceiling towering above her, Faye was reminded for a moment of the antiquities of the San Mateo *finca*, only with a thousand times more atmosphere.

The others caught her up and from the gateway they made their way up to the extreme crown of the bluff. It was thrilling to imagine the all-conquering Moors up here, languishing in Eastern splendour so many centuries ago, as one examined the remains of crumbling walls and traces of a luxurious layout in what must have been truly an invincible position.

Faye was musing over a big stone trough in the ground which could have, at one time, held the Moors' water supply, when a tiny scream from Greta drew her attention. The others were standing at the edge of the bluff, on the opposite side to the way they had come up.

'Come over here and have a look at this, Faye,' Greta called delightedly, holding tight to her husband's sleeve. Faye swung over the springy turf towards them. She hadn't noticed how the ground sloped towards the edge until Brent, standing beside the Conde and Carmina, stepped forward to thrust out a steadying arm. 'Hold on. There's no wall here.'

Faye soon saw the reason for the others' awe. Beyond the edge of the bluff, the ground dropped sharply away, disappearing for ever, it seemed, until one's eye, over the terrified pounding of one's heart, came up against the misty green of a wide valley somewhere down there milleniums of feet below. Almost underneath one's feet the sky stretched in an infinity of space.

Greta, revelling in Faye's look of amused alarm, gasped with lurid enjoyment, 'Isn't it just too horrifying!'

'Ghastly.' Faye grimaced, and nodded across to the crumbling walls of the stronghold. 'The other side's probably more interesting. I wonder if we can see the *finca* from here.'

'There's a lookout tower,' the Conde offered, delighted at the stir among the ladies at the giddy heights. 'Unfortunately, with this heat haze the far distances may be a little indistinct.'

'Lead the way, Enrique,' Brent said lazily, keeping a firm grip on Faye's arm. 'We'll be right behind.'

Far too eager to wait for the Conde, Greta hurried ahead of him, and with Bart in tow was the first to experience the spine-chilling sensation to be found inside the sole remaining structure, a small square-built room in line with the crenellated battlements walling in the edge of the bluff.

'Ooh! Don't go in there!' she said, ushering Faye inside with a look of enraptured shock on her face. 'It's awful!'

The Conde, who had preceded Faye into the look-out tower along with Carmina, gestured proudly. Faye couldn't quite grasp what it was that had so stunned Greta, but as she came up to the wall opening she could understand the other woman's comic fear.

The window was tall and wide and came barely to her shins, so that she had a feeling of standing poised and unprotected over a view of the sheer cliff wall of the bluff. It descended sickeningly down ... down, hundreds and thousands of feet below, until the gaze was lost among strewn granite boulders in seemingly subterranean depths.

Brent put an arm across the opening, and to distract her hypnotised stare he nodded into the distance and drawled with idle humour, 'Somewhere out there is the famed *finca* of San Mateo.'

Faye lifted her gaze, rooted by the fantastic beauty of the panorama. Half the island was spread out before her, the gossamer haze under which it lay did little to mar its shimmering magnificence. As though in a paper-chase the scattering of white villages littered the foot of the dark green slopes, others were strung out across the tremendous bosom of the plain like a chunky sea-shell necklace.

They could see clear all the way to Palma, and up the wavy indentation of the coastline where the sea lay like molten silver beneath the mist. The Conde pointed over her shoulder to a dark sugar-loaf hummock in the immediate distance, and she couldn't believe it when he told her that they were the tall pine-clad slopes which sheltered his house. Try as they would they couldn't distinguish any sign of San Mateo in the vast patchwork of the island spread out below.

Carmina lost interest and the Conde followed her out. With the warm mountain breezes wafting through the opening Faye would have loved to go on musing on her surroundings; picturing a bearded Moor striding back and forth in here, and keeping a sharp look out over land and sea for the enemy. But left alone with Brent she didn't trust herself, and when he guided her away she went with him meekly.

Among the others, however, it was easier to let herself go. She said eagerly, swinging alongside Brent, 'There's a little white church at the very edge of the bluff. Enrique pointed it out to me from the *finca*. Can't we go to see it?'

Brent's grin as he watched her youthful enthusiasm was tolerant. 'We've come this far. We might as well see all there is to see.'

The others followed them along the winding paths, Greta flushed with ecstatic nervousness and Bart grumbling noisily and enjoying every moment of it. The Conde, walking a little behind Carmina, brought up the rear.

The church was obviously the focal point of interest for visitors to this fortress in the sky, for here several sightseers were wandering leisurely over the springy turf at the furthermost point of the plateau. Besides the little indoor altar with its brightly coloured decor, vases of flowers and gleaming icons, there was an adjoining stone-built cottage which served as an overnight rest-house, a place to buy drinks and tourists' gifts, and generally to put one's feet up. It was really like the corner of some Spanish village with its grape loggia, tethered dogs and old stone drinking well. Shades of the courtyard at the *finca*! Faye mused with a twinkle.

Bart brought out a tray of drinks, for it had been hot and thirsty work climbing to the summit. Faye was the first to finish hers. There was a walled-in platform over-looking the panorama and she went over to get a closer look. The Conde, glass in hand, strolled over to join her, followed by Carmina.

Faye gave her attention to the view. They were too far away from the edge of the plateau up here to see more than the great bowl of blue sky and blur of greenery below, but Faye took deep gulps of the cool, washed mountain air and turned her face to the breeze.

The Conde eyed her sparkle with his teasing dark gaze and asked, 'Was I right when I told you the view surpassed all others?'

'Indubitably!' Faye laughed up at him. 'I wouldn't have missed it for the world. I must take another peep in the lookout tower before I go down.'

Brent finished his cigarette and strolled over ready for the journey back the way they had come. Greta and Bart had already started out, but Faye had promised herself a look at the water wheel over the well. 'How does it work?' she asked Brent, fiddling with the old iron handle.

'I imagine we turn it here,' he said after studying the ancient contraption. He coaxed it into motion and up came the battered steel cups, filled to overflowing with crystal clear mountain water. 'Want to try it?' he asked with his blue gleam.

Faye eyed the cups, dented with age and use, and with a little grimace laughed gaily. 'Not just now, thank you.'

The others had been gone for some time when they finally started out on the downward route. But Faye didn't mind. Brent's company was heady indeed, making her want to prolong these moments alone with him; besides, the paths were easy to follow over the crown of the plateau, among twisted trees and over turf and granite stretches. They traversed the sloping route in something almost like companionable silence,

Brent giving her a hand here and there over the steep drops in the paths.

When they reached the level of the Moorish stronghold the other four were dotted around engrossed in their various occupations. Greta was sat on a rock shaking the gravel from her sandals, and Bart was rewarding himself with a fresh pipeful of tobacco while discussing some angle of the view with the Conde. Carmina was bent—an odd posture for her—trailing her fingers through the water in the stone trough and gazing down into its dark depths with that enigmatic, sphinxlike smile stamped on her hard features.

Faye ought to have been warned, but she wasn't. Her heart and mind were full of Brent's nearness, and she wanted only to wring the last ounce of sweetness out of the day. She was intent on recapturing those moments in which she had stood with him in the watch-tower, and thrilling once again to the stunning panorama spread out below.

As everyone gathered together for the final descent she hurried along and dived inside the watch-tower for what she told herself would be one last quick look.

It was dark inside the ruined enclosure, and her gaze was dimmed to the scattering of rocks and broken slabs of stone in the far corners by the sun-brilliant scene of blue sky and green island framed in the lookout window.

Faye didn't see the thin slab of stone which had been positioned with sinister precision in the shadows beneath the opening. Nor did she know it had been precariously balanced with a roll of rock beneath so that the merest weight would tip it forward. She rushed in and hurried to the window, then as her foot touched the false platform of rock a piercing scream was wrenched from her.

The ground seemed to give way beneath her feet. She saw herself hurtling out of the window, saw the cruel, jagged rocks waiting to receive her mangled body like a sea of granite vultures.

Without knowing it she had flung out her arms. Her wrists, bruised and grazed against the thick stone walls of the window, impeded her flight, and together with Brent's lightning movement—for he had been no more than a step away from her outside—she cheated death and the waiting rocks below by a blood-chilling hair's breadth.

Brent's arms gripped her. Faye knew that he had seen the faulty slab structure in the shadows at their feet as he held her white and shaking form close against him, saying hoarsely, 'Good God! What are you trying to do, give us all the fright of our lives?'

The others crowded in as she was led out, and made way among murmurs of sympathy. 'Poor darling!' Greta was genuinely concerned. 'I knew at the start it wasn't safe to go too near the edge in there. I bet you're not the first one to get such a fright.'

Brent made no comment on this or any of the other consoling remarks which were forthcoming. He was still eyeing the pale form beneath his gaze. A grim look on his face, his arms still locked tight around her, he said, 'Faye's had a bad scare. I'm taking her home.'

CHAPTER TWELVE

ALL was quiet around the *finca*. Ana had gone off to gossip with her daughter in the village, and Anofre was busy with the autumn ploughing in the valley. Apart from the impatient 'Whoa's and *'Aribe!'* with which he smote his cantankerous mule, all was peaceful and calm.

From her seat under the shady umbrella overlooking the valley Faye could see the slate blue mountains,

168

solid and shadowless against the apricot flush of late afternoon. Her bandaged wrists still throbbed painfully, and her eyes were big and dark with shock in her pale face.

Enrique had paid her a call during the afternoon. He had come up the hill on foot, a bunch of the field flowers in his hand, and for once entirely on his own. Faye didn't know how much he knew of Carmina's dangerous tactics in trying to get rid of her; although there was a sheepish look in his rakish dark eyes, his manner had been playfully solicitous, and he had left when he had satisfied himself that all was well at the *finca*.

Greta had sent her some fruit and flowers with Brent. *Brent*. Faye still shuddered when she recalled her descent down the mountain with him yesterday. Though he had assisted her with all gentleness down the steep sloping paths, she had sensed the icy violence in him, a towering anger which she knew he had held in check solely by superhuman control.

It wasn't until after their final descent in the car, executed with iron control, and their tense race through the countryside back to San Mateo, that he had seemed gradually to regain a hold on his fury. He had turned into the side lane calmly, and brought the car to a whispering halt in the courtyard.

Her hands clasped in her lap, Faye gave a long quivering sigh and stared at the mountains.

She was feeling stronger a few days later when the Templetons dropped in. Brent brought drinks out to the terrace and the four of them sat and chatted desultorily. No one broached the subject of Faye's 'accident', the general opinion being that the less said about the unfortunate episode, the better. Of the same mind, Faye had pushed the unpleasant incident out of her thoughts.

After sitting for a while the men went off to indulge

in masculine pursuits, while Greta and Faye sipped their drinks and gazed at the view. Or at least that was Faye's occupation. She knew that Greta's searching blue glance rested on her for most of the time, but with a desire to keep the conversation going she asked smilingly, 'How are things at the hotel? Still busy?'

'Business is slacking off a bit now, thank heaven,' Greta grimaced good-humouredly. 'Bart and I are not sorry. We're dying for a break.'

Faye nodded. It had only just occurred to her that all during these past months while she had been battling with the various minor crises in her life, the Templetons had been hard at it, dealing with family bookings, crowded dining rooms, staff shortages and all the rest of the tiring work that went into the running of a hotel. They took a breather only when she and Brent and the others had dropped in for a couple of hours in the afternoon, or when they drove out here for a change of scene. For them it would have been a long summer.

She said, 'Will you be taking a holiday?'

Greta nodded. 'We usually go away for about a month. We'll leave the hotel ticking over with a winter staff, and get back in time to prepare for the Christmas rush. Bart fancies the Canary Islands, but I'd like to go somewhere further afield.'

Greta paused. She looked as though she would have liked to ask Faye what she would be doing, but instead she said impulsively, 'You haven't had a meal at the hotel yet. Why not come over about midday tomorrow for lunch?'

Taking it as a kind of farewell gesture, Faye pondered and then agreed to the suggestion. They were talking on a different subject when the men returned. A short while later she went out to the lane entrance to wave the Templetons off.

The next day, driving out to Porto Cristo, Faye half

regretted accepting Greta's invitation to lunch. She felt jaded both in mind and body and in no mood for the gay atmosphere of the hotel; however, knowing that there was no going back on her promise, she made her way out to the coast with weary resignation. She had put on a simple oatmeal linen dress, and an amber ribbon held her hair in a burnished coil on one shoulder.

The town was quieter than she remembered it. She drove up past the beach and parked her car in the now almost deserted *calle*. There were one or two guests in the lounge of the Hotel Azalea, and more could be seen strolling in the cliff grounds beyond the windows.

Greta came to meet her and led her through into the Templetons' private abode. 'Brent's here,' she said, shooting a look at Faye just as her eyes met a pair of familiar blue ones inside the chintzy drawing room.

Brent looked as startled to see her as she was to see him, but Greta fussed around the table beside the window with a decidedly guilty air. 'Bart and I were planning to join you, but we're absolutely run off our feet today. So much work!' She threw up her hands, forgetting that they all knew that the hotel was practically empty. 'Anyway, I'm sure you two will manage alone.'

Faye watched her go out leaving them to it. Dear, kindly Greta! She had slyly arranged all this. But she knew nothing of the rift between herself and Brent.

She turned and met his blue gaze across the table, and he came and held the chair for her to sit down. When he looked at her like that, she could almost forgive him the colossal hurt he had caused her, linking her with the Conde all these weeks.

He took his seat across the table from her. In working attire, cream shirt of tropical tailored design and light slacks, he had obviously been caught out like her. He looked older in the light from the window, she could see a stray grey hair glinting here and there at his temples. And gone was the mocking humour of the old days. His rugged features were stamped with an expression of careworn maturity.

Had she done that to him? Her throat constricted as she dragged her gaze away with an effort.

The window looked out on to a private patio garden where pastel-coloured hydrangeas flowered in gaily painted pots along the low wall. The brilliance of red geraniums came through the shade of overhanging greenery.

A Spanish waiter served them with the courses of the meal, cooked in the impeccable style of the Hotel Azalea. In an intimacy they had never known before, Brent performed the task of shelling the dressed lobster on their plates while Faye took it on herself to attend to his wine glass, and later filled his cup from the elegant silver coffee pot.

Afterwards they sat on the huge chintz-covered sofa facing the white carved fireplace. Brent lit up a cigarette and they talked. The Conde, the *finca*, all were forgotten as Faye told him about her family in England, about the tea rooms her parents ran in a celebrated beauty spot in the south, and the two aunts who came to help out in the summer.

Brent related his various experiences during his travels around Europe designing golf courses. He told her how he had first become interested in making a career for himself as a golf architect.

They learned more about each other in a short space of time than they had done in all the months living under the same roof at San Mateo.

After a while Brent stubbed out his cigarette and said, 'Fancy a drive?'

'Yes, if you do.' Faye couldn't help it if her eyes were shining.

They went out and through the hotel to Brent's car. The world outside seemed flooded, brilliant with sunshine; a warmer, gayer world than Faye had ever known as Brent escorted her, a possessive arm drawing her close to him.

They drove past the beach and out of town. It wasn't long before Faye realised they were making for La Zarzamora and when they arrived at the golf course, she was stunned at the changes which had taken place since her first and last visit in early February. Gone were the barren stretches. Now emerald green turf carpeted the undulating distances. There were blue pools reflecting the soft October light, luxuriant tree banks, and gay flags dotting the greens.

They drove along metalled roads towards the club-house, a stone and wood-panelled dream with a low red-tiled roof, surrounded by rose gardens and green lawns. Faye wandered along the paths beside Brent. They went indoors where workmen were putting the finishing touches to the tiled walls and bar. The men watched *el maestro* move outside again, and speculated on his interest in the girl at his side.

Faye shaded her eyes to admire the surrounding views. All was tranquil. Nothing moved for miles over the rolling green stretches, only the occasional twitter of a bird in flight fell on the stillness.

There were no opulent cars parked here today, but unhappily Faye couldn't obliterate from the scene the shimmering white structure in the distance.

As though he knew something of the direction of her gaze Brent said easily, 'Shall we go and pay a call at the villa?'

They drove over the smooth route and parked outside the beautiful old porticoed entrance. Inside, a breathless hush hung over the palm tree-shaded enclosure with its fluted balconies and trailing blood-red hibiscus.

Brent led the way through the dim indoors. He nodded and had a word, here and there, with the elderly figures who sat poring over heavy books, or dozing over the daily paper; outdoors they made their way towards the swimming pool, where the obvious head of the household, a white-haired figure with hawk-like features, fierce eyes and a gentle mouth, sat wrapped in a light wool rug.

He greeted Brent warmly and invited Faye to sit beside him. She thought his voice, as he spoke in pure Spanish of the old school, was the most beautiful she had ever heard.

As they sat sipping drinks served by a grizzle-haired butler, Faye felt puzzled. The villa was nothing like the way she remembered it. The atmosphere reminded one of the exclusive and staid interior of a club for retired gentlemen.

Unable to contain her curiosity, she said to the old man at her side, 'It's all so different from the last time I came. There were girls around my own age here beside the pool. Do they still come over from Barcelona?'

The old man laughed. 'Grandchildren today want to be where the fun is. The girls came over once or twice, but they prefer the beaches of Marbella and the gay night life of the Costa del Sol to languishing in a lifeless old villa.'

Faye sipped her drink and felt the glow spread inwardly. So there had been no one here all summer except the elderly members of the family. As she swallowed on a surge of ridiculous happiness she came up against Brent's blue gaze. Had he wanted her to know this?

After a pleasant interlude they took their leave of the venerable old figure beside the pool and went back out to the car. They cruised over the golf course routes out to the circular country road. As they linked up with the main road that would take them back to San Mateo, Faye had a sudden thought. Brent grinned, 'Don't worry. I'll ring Bart and ask him to get one of the hotel men to drive your car over.' Faye smiled and relaxed again.

As his car purred over the road Brent said, 'Another couple of days and my work will be finished at La Zarzamora. I've accepted a commission in the Bahamas.'

The Bahamas! Faye was breathless.

He went on, 'I thought I'd round things off with a little farewell gathering in my rooms. I've invited the Templetons and the Conde and Carmina,' he turned to look at her, 'for old times' sake.'

'Of course,' Faye smiled. Nothing could penetrate the secure, cosy feeling which Brent's nearness gave her. It had been a heavenly, heavenly afternoon and her heart was walking on air. Whatever Brent said was fine by her.

He dropped her off in the courtyard and reversed, saying that he had to get back to work. She watched him drive away with shining eyes.

Ana and Anofre were invited upstairs for a drink on the night of Brent's party. The catering had been done by a Llosaya firm specialising in continental delicacies, but so no one's feelings would be hurt, Ana had been allowed to contribute a tray of her Majorcan pastries and Anofre, quite surprisingly smart in his Sunday suit, supplied a bottle of local San Mateo wine. The couple stayed for about an hour, not entirely at ease among the bright lights and sophisticated chatter, after which they shyly took their leave to hurry to the more homely realms of tugging grandchildren and family gossip in the village.

Faye saw them out to the top of the stairs above the courtyard, then returned across the dimly-lit salon. Light flooded out from the doorway of Brent's apartment; she could see the fire blazing merrily in the grate, lit specially for the occasion, the armchairs and carpets, just inside where the festivities were being held.

How well she remembered the scene. It took her back to that first rainy, squally night when she had arrived, a dripping, muddy wreck after her journey out from England, and Brent had stood framed in this very doorway. What a lifetime away it all seemed now. A happy flush was on her cheeks as she went inside and closed the door.

Across the room, through the big curtainless windows, it was not yet quite dark. Ostrich feather clouds of deep salmon pink were strewn down the pure turquoise sky. Towards the mountains the sun was setting in a blaze of unbelievable October glory.

Inside the room, the sideboard was littered with the left-overs of food and drink, music played from a small radio. There was a little smoke from Bart's pipe, and Brent's cigarettes.

Faye felt content. She had dressed simply in a powder blue dress and left her hair to fall loose on her shoulders. Brent was dressed casually, but expensively, the way she remembered him best, soft shoes, tailored slacks and woollen shirt which showed to perfection his muscular arms and shoulders.

She hadn't realised how much she was giving away in her gaze until Greta came up beside her to fill her glass at the sideboard. But Greta being Greta she made no direct comment on the fact that she had glimpsed Faye's heart in her eyes. She approached it by way of another topic. 'Isn't it exciting!' she gushed, frothing soda water into her glass. 'We're off to the Bahamas for our holidays. Bart likes the idea now that he knows Brent's going to be out there.' Greta's whimsical blue gaze came over the top of her glass. She said, experimenting with the flavour of her drink, 'Wouldn't it be wonderful if the four of us could meet up in Nassau?'

Faye didn't trust herself to reply. Instead she viewed the others around the room, a little tune playing in her heart, while Greta chatted on about inconsequential things.

Bart was puffing his pipe beside Carmina. An uncomplicated soul, he could get along with anyone, perhaps because he didn't bother to work at it. Bart was the only one with whom Carmina relaxed sufficiently to allow a smile to flit across her aquiline features from time to time.

The Andalusian woman made a striking figure tonight. She had dressed with care in a tight-fitting black dress whose deep frills from the hips were lined with crimson satin; a silk shawl trailing long crimson fringes was draped loosely over her shoulders. Glittering combs held back her blacker-than-black hair, and loops of ebony dangling at her ears matched the big round beads resting on her ample bosom.

Though she appeared to be listening to every word that Bart was saying to her, her eyes seemed to be trained across the room, pleading with the Conde to notice her.

Enrique, tall in a white outdated suit which somehow flattered his rakish appearance, might have been aware of her presence. But if he was, he disguised it admirably as he stood making idle chat with Brent.

Greta decided she would like a cigarette and went over to beg one from Brent, and Faye was fiddling with the radio looking for more non-stop music when Enrique came over to curl an arm round her waist. He might have tried to monopolise her company, but he was given no opportunity tonight. It was Brent who drifted over and, his head close to hers, found the music she was looking for. And it was Brent who, whenever the rhythm was right, drew her against him and drifted round idly to the music in the subdued lighting near the windows.

It was on one such occasion, when his cheek brushed close to hers, that he whirled her gently towards the open doorway of the adjoining room, leaving the others to their drinks and their chat and the music.

In the shadows lit by an occasional table lamp, in the room that was Brent's den, Faye felt his arms tighten about her, his lips brush her throat. She thought she would die from the aching sweetness of his nearness, and suddenly, on an impulse, she broke away from him with a little laugh and whirled away to explore the room.

She wanted to know all there was to know about Brent. She skipped, touching the books on the workbench lightly, and ran a finger over the heavy ash-tray on the window-sill. There was evidence of packing; suitcases littered the floor and oddments piled ready for stowing away made a trail through an open doorway and along a carpeted corridor.

Brent followed her with a lazy smile. Too shy to turn to him yet, she whirled along the wall-lit corridor, peeping into this room and that, laughter on her lips. One door she opened turned out to be no more than an old closet cluttered with junk. But wait a minute! Weren't those canvases stacked against the wall?

Intrigued, she stooped and tugged one out, holding it to the light for inspection. Laughter bubbled from her as she imagined she had stumbled on a secret hobby of Brent's. Then she gazed at the subject. It looked vaguely familiar.

The laughter cracked in her throat, and the radiant smile curving her lips dried to become a puzzled and horrible grimace as she read the signature. *F. Chalmers.* She felt as though she had stepped into some grotesque nightmare where nothing made sense.

Frantically, to rid herself of the feeling, she began to tug at more pictures, pulling them out one by one and flinging them to the light. They were all the same. The black scrawl laughed out at her with demoniacal sameness, *F. Chalmers ... F. Chalmers....*

Brent had quickened his step, but he was too late. On her knees she stared up at him. The light of accusation in her eyes, she whispered, 'It was you! You're the one who's been buying my paintings in Llosaya?'

'Yes,' Brent said levelly.

Faye was on her feet, hot blazing tears rushing to her eyes as the curtain of truth was lifted. How could she bear it?—Brent putting up with her insufferable, strutting behaviour, knowing that her talents as a painter were negligible. And worse! Oh, a thousand times worse! A sob rose in her throat. To know that Brent had been financing her, while believing that she was striving hard to engineer a marriage of convenience between herself and the Conde, was the final humiliation.

Wounded and angry beyond words, the force of her torn emotions gave her wings as she rushed along the corridor. Brent called after her sharply, 'Faye! Wait!'

But her slim form was much more manoeuvreable among the furniture of the lamp-lit room than his.

She reached the brilliantly lit doorway. The tears dry on her cheeks, a smile pasted on her face to hide the brittle light in her eyes she cried shakily, 'Listen, everybody. I've got a special announcement to make. If Enrique will have me,' she ran over to link her arm in his, 'we're to be married right away!'

An electric silence fell on the room. The radio went on playing as though in another world; Greta's jaw dropped. Brent stood grey-faced in the doorway across the room.

Always oblivious to atmosphere, Bart was the first one to come round after the outburst. 'Well, congratulations, you two. This calls for a special toast.'

Faye turned to the sideboard behind her, the Conde close beside her. She had seen the leap of triumph in his dark eyes, and tried to still her trembling hands as she reached for the bottle of wine.

But the toast was never made.

A sudden shattering of glass made Faye spin round. She was in time to see Carmina's wine glass splinter into fragments in the fireplace. From where she had hurled it, close beside Faye, Carmina's harsh voice smouldered, 'I for one do not offer my good wishes for such a union!'

A curse fell from the lips of the Andalusian woman, but what rooted everyone in the room was the sudden flash of steel in her hands; a cruel, glinting knife which she must have produced from somewhere on her person.

The shock of what was going to happen before their very eyes turned everyone to stone. Brent might have reached Faye's side, but he was over on the far side of the room. A million obstacles separated them.

It was his leap forward which galvanised Faye into movement. Everything was happening in the fraction of a second as she backed away and clawed at the door behind her. It was slightly ajar. She felt the blow of it wind the Andalusian woman as she flung it open, and outside in the salon she hesitated wildly. The thought of the outside door and the steep flight of steps paralysed her with fear; she ran instead towards the corner entrance. It was her undoing.

Across the sparsely lit space Carmina, swift of foot despite her heavier carriage, flitted after her like a swooping black raven. They reached the opening almost at the same time, then in one rapid movement Carmina turned and slammed the heavy, creaking door behind them. Faye's blood turned to ice as she heard the key turning in the lock seconds before Brent's fists came hammering on the door. 'Carmina! Car-min-a!' His voice shook with desperation.

Above the fearful thumping on the door she could hear Carmina's laboured breathing. It was dark, but there was enough light from under the door and from fan-lights reflecting the stars to make out the six-inch blade of steel, and Carmina's blazing black eyes, jet hard and aflame with passionate hatred.

Her lips drawn back from her teeth, she advanced, sure of her ground now. She fixed Faye with a look of withering disdain and spat, 'Do you think I would turn Enrique over to you when the love I hold for him is a thousand times greater than the puny affection you profess? Do you imagine that I have lowered myself to do the work of a servant—I, Carmina del Flores de Argalis,' she flung back her head with arrogant pride, 'to keep Enrique alive for you?'

Distantly aware of the wild hammering on the stout wood panels, the cries of Bart and Greta and the Conde begging her to open the door, Faye stood rooted and watched Carmina's aquiline, parchment-like features contort with contempt as she advanced. 'Oh, I've watched you all these weeks trying to wheedle your way into Enrique's affections. I've watched you and laughed.' She threw back her head and gave a shout of arrogant laughter, then swift as a predatory eagle she brought her black eyes down to nail Faye with her gaze. 'How can you, a feeble, vapid child from the north, know anything of the fire and the passion that is Spain? The blood that ties Enrique to his own kind—to me!' She flung up her head and fixed Faye with a look of blistering scorn.

Faye's legs were threatening to buckle under her. Her heart was pounding with fear. She fell back along the corridor as Carmina came on slowly, flaying her with her tongue, pouring out the venom she had withheld for months, knife raised ready for the final act of contempt.

Bart's voice, along with the Conde's, still pleaded at the door. They had found some kind of battering ram and were raining heavy blows ... thud ... thud ... thud against the solid surface. It was old, and it might splinter in time, but Faye knew it would be too late for her.

She slumped against the wall of the corridor, terror freezing her. She could go no further. Carmina advanced, silent now, triumph already blazing in her black eyes. Driven by the primitive forces which lie hidden beneath the civilised veneer in so many of her race, she flung back her knife hand ready to bring it down with the swiftness her hate demanded.

Faye shrank into herself, hypnotised by the sudden flash of steel. She wanted to scream, but no sound escaped her fear-parched throat. She prepared to slump to the floor, the glint of steel poised above her breast. Then into the blood-chilling moment a voice from the shadows close at hand rent the air. 'Carmina!'

The sound of her name in her ear was enough to freeze the love-crazed Carmina into immobility. A sinister, predatory figure, she swung her puzzled glance into the darkness. It was long enough. Faye felt a hand grip her. Brent! The next moment she was jerked into his arms where he enfolded her tightly against him, muttering down at her in cracked, shaky tones, 'You crazy little fool!'

The Andalusian woman shrank back as behind her the door splintered with a mighty crack and gave way. As it was flung wide the three who had been locked on the outside rushed forward with white faces. The Conde's was the most haggard of all and gently he led the weeping Carmina away. Greta eyed Faye clinging to Brent, his arms secure about her, and with a dry, worn little smile she said, 'Let's go home, Bart.'

A cool wind blew across the south terrace. The gay beach umbrella, faded by a perpetual bleaching under the summer sun, flapped a little forlornly now above a view of dull, ploughed fields and bare trees and vines.

Faye dismantled the umbrella and began to tie it up along with the rest of the outdoor furniture, ready for delivery back to the Templetons. Her cases were packed and ready in the courtyard. She had had enough of San Mateo.

Ana and Anofre had gone off with vegetables and fruit to the town market and wouldn't be back until late afternoon. But what did that matter? She had said her goodbyes.

She had made a neat bundle of the umbrella when a sound came up the cart track from the valley and dully it registered on her tired brain that it was the Conde's car.

As a token gesture she showed herself at the end of the terrace. Enrique was on his own. The wind blew his hair as he strode towards her; it blurred his humble smile, and flapped his thin suit, giving him a shabby look.

'Faye!' He took her hand as they walked on to the terrace. They sat down, and still holding her hand he said, 'I've come to tell you that Carmina and I are going to be married.'

'I'm glad,' Faye dropped a hand over his and smiled. 'She loves you in a very special way. I'm sure you'll find great happiness together.'

The Conde looked at her, a faint glimmering of the old mischief in his eyes. 'I don't regret having made your acquaintance.'

He rose and kissed her hand with feeling. 'I'm on my way to town to book ferry tickets. We'll take the night boat to Alicante, then motor down through Malaga to Carmina's family.'

Faye walked to the terrace end with him.

'*Adios, querida.*' His tones were soft. He lingered momentarily, and Faye smiled.

'Goodbye, Enrique, and good luck.'

The Conde gave a shrug, but she noticed as he made

his way to his car that he didn't once turn back to look out over the valley at the vast lands of San Mateo.

She went back to tying up the folding chairs and heard the exchange of car horns as Enrique drove out along the lane.

Her hands trembled at her task. She hadn't seen Brent since last night, when she had torn herself out of his arms and fled to her room.

His apartment was all locked up, his personal possessions packed and ready for shipment in the garage. She knew that he had gone down to Llosaya to hand over the keys to the lawyer.

She heard his car crunching into the courtyard now. She didn't show herself. Brent seemed to know where she was. She heard his footsteps on the turf behind her, and now, she felt steady and calm.

She knew he was watching her work with scissors and string. He said presently, 'José Andrés tells me you're turning San Mateo over to the state.'

'That's right,' Faye nodded coolly. 'I had a talk with him this morning. Apparently the government would welcome the idea of turning the *finca* and grounds into a *parador*, a state-owned inn. I'm told that the Rodriguez couple have long since wanted to retire into the village where they have just enough land to keep them occupied, and José Andrés is letting me have my fare back to England. So!' she shrugged. 'There appear to be no problems.'

By the sound of his voice when he spoke again Brent seemed to have drawn nearer. 'I met the Conde in the lane.'

'Oh.' Faye snipped at the string carefully.

'Congratulations were in order, it seemed. He told me that he and Carmina are going to be married.'

'That's right.' Faye folded another chair on to the table.

'You don't seem terribly cut up about it,' came the

voice behind her.

'I'm not.'

She heard his low curse of exasperation. 'For pity's sake stop snipping!' His hand on her wrist, he pulled her to him with a tortured look. 'Come here and tell me you don't care a hang for the Conde or San Mateo.'

'I never have,' she returned staring at him blandly.

He gazed hard at her. 'I know last night was just a silly act of bravado, but what about all the other times, when you were over at the Conde's house, and tearing round the countryside with him in his time-bomb of a car?'

'That was done to deflate your ego. How was I to know you would put the construction you did on a harmless flirtation?' She faced him squarely, a stormy light in her tawny eyes. 'Do you regard every woman you meet as a potential gold-digger?'

Brent's eyes narrowed over her. 'When one of them stands to win or lose a few thousand acres of valuable land, I'd say the chances are fifty-fifty that she'll plump for the fortune.'

'Then all *I* can say,' she flared, 'is that there's a lot to be desired in the company you keep!'

His fingers, gripping her, slowly relaxed. A weary grin tugged at the corners of his mouth. 'I'm willing to admit I was wrong. But why didn't you put me straight?'

'That was a pretty nasty accusation you made.' Faye lifted her chin. 'It took some living down. Then I found out that José Andrés and everyone else was thinking the same, and I saw red.'

Brent eyed her with his blue gleam. 'And, because you were bristling with pride, you preferred to run the gauntlet of Carmina's jealous hate, rather than have it out with me?'

'I was too miserable to think about Carmina.' Faye felt herself softening. 'It all started off so innocently.

The Conde proposed to me in a roundabout way on our second meeting.'

'The cunning old fox,' Brent glinted. 'I suppose he was after a slice of the cake?'

'I didn't take him seriously.' Now Faye's eyes gleamed. 'But I thought it would be fun to pretend that I did to take you down a peg or two.'

Brent's grin broadened. 'You were struck on me from the start?'

'From the start,' Faye admitted it now.

'I guess I was smitten in the same way.' His humorous gaze darkening, Brent pulled her close and murmured, 'It hasn't been much fun for either of us. What say we bury the hatchet?'

'Do you have to ask me that?'

He kissed her hungrily, but with a tenderness which, loving him as she did, she lingeringly returned.

Later he said, his head close to hers, 'I was beginning to get the feeling that I meant more to you than San Mateo, and I had an idea I could call your bluff. I arranged the party and planned to announce our engagement to the others, but you found the paintings and turned the tables on me.'

Faye winced up at him. 'How will I ever live it down? I was so horribly stuffy and cocksure, and you knew my pictures were worthless.'

Brent smiled. 'To me your paintings are the most wonderful in the world.'

'Just the same,' she slanted him a wry look, 'I think I'll take up some other occupation.'

'How does wife to a successful golf architect strike you?' he asked, his lips brushing her cheek.

'I have to admit the idea appeals.' Thoughtfully she fiddled with the lapel of his doe-skin leather jacket. 'I've a feeling I wasn't very good at hiding my money problems.'

'You were a walking streak of independence,' Brent

grinned, 'but it wasn't difficult to see you were scratching along on a farm diet. I spoke to Greta about it.'

That day at the pool when she was almost at the end of her tether. How well Faye remembered it.

'She told me you were having difficulty in finding your feet as a painter,' Brent went on, 'so I went down to town and played the art-conscious tourist. Nobody knew. I thought I pulled it off rather well.'

She gave him a mock-scolding look. 'And all the time you believed I was making a play for the Conde.'

Brent shrugged. 'The way it looked you were set on owning San Mateo.' He held her close to him. 'I spent some sleepless nights wondering what Carmina would think up next to get you out of the way.'

'You suspected something?' Faye glanced up at him. Brent nodded.

'The day you took a nose-dive down the hillside. I went down later to take a look at your car, and I discovered that the brakes had been tampered with.'

Faye shuddered. 'Poor Carmina! I'm afraid the Conde and I drove her beyond the limits of her endurance. Last night. . . .' she buried her face in his jacket as the awful nightmare flooded back, '. . . how did you manage to reach us?'

'I climbed out of a window in my apartment and went over the roof.' Brent gripped her. 'I took a gamble that there would be some way in, and I spotted a kind of walled-in courtyard with a lot of green stuff growing. I shinned down a drainpipe and found a way in through a window at the side.'

Through the L-shaped room! Faye smiled back her surprise, and examined him closely. 'That was a dangerous thing to do. Are you sure you're all right?'

'A cricked ankle,' Brent grinned, and dropped his lips in her hair. 'Nothing that a nice long honeymoon won't cure.'

Faye's eyes twinkled over the delicate pink on her

cheeks.

'That is, if you fancy a long spell out in the Bahamas with a villa laid on for the duration,' his lips touched her ear.

'Sounds like heaven!' Faye murmured.

They woke up to the time at last and Brent glanced over at the chairs. 'I'll put this lot in the car with the rest of our stuff and we'll go and tell the Templetons the good news. After that I'm driving you to Palma to buy a ring befitting the future Mrs Garrett, then I fancy taking a look at this tea rooms beauty spot you were telling me about, before we fly out to the Bahamas.'

Faye sparkled happily. She would like nothing better than to show off Brent to her family at home. She watched him stack the chairs and thinking of the two who, next to Brent, had become very dear to her, she mused humorously, 'I don't think it will come as any surprise to Greta, us two showing up. I've a feeling she's been rooting for you ever since we met.'

'Greta's an old mate,' Brent smiled. 'If she wants to paint the town puce and polka dots in Nassau that's fine by me.'

With a load under one arm, his other arm hugged her close to him as they made their way laughingly into the courtyard.

Brent fondled a dog here and there in passing as he transferred their suitcases over to the car. Faye watched the whining friendly shapes with a damp eye; she had a feeling they were going to know more freedom in their new home. The sight of her little battered car wrenched at her heart. Perhaps someone would find a use for it.

When everything was packed and Brent was locking the car boot, Faye gazed up at the tall buttresses of the *finca* and over the roof-top towards the grand salons. Brent said, taking her arm, 'We'll come back one day when it's a *parador*. Look in on the Rodriguez couple and maybe spend a second honeymoon here.'

Faye let him help her into her seat. It wasn't exactly with a feeling of sadness that she had gazed towards the mansion-like proportions of the *finca*. She had been thinking of those other presences there; not altogether hostile perhaps. It was uncanny how Brent had managed to make his way unhampered to her rescue last night, through the little courtyard and the L-shaped room. . . .

As they drove away, her head on Brent's shoulder, a small smile played around Faye's lips. Somehow she had a feeling that her grandmother approved her choice.

Harlequin

the unique monthly magazine packed with good things for Harlequin readers!

A Complete Harlequin Novel

You'll get hours of reading enjoyment from Harlequin fiction. Along with a variety of specially selected short stories, every issue of the magazine contains a complete romantic novel.

Readers' Page

A lively forum for exchanging news and views from Harlequin readers. If you would like to share your thoughts, we'd love to hear from you.

Arts and Crafts

Unusual handicraft articles are a fascinating feature of Harlequin magazine. You'll enjoy making your own gifts and indulging your creativity when you use these always clear and easy-to-follow instructions.

Author's Own Story . . .

Now, meet the very real people who create the romantic world of Harlequin! In these unusual author profiles a well-known author tells you her own personal story.

Harlequin Cookery

Temptingly delicious dishes, plain and fancy, from all over the world. Recreate these dishes from tested, detailed recipes, for your family and friends.

Faraway Places . . .

Whether it's to remind you of places you've enjoyed visiting, or to learn about places you're still hoping to see, you'll find the travel articles informative and interesting — and just perfect for armchair travelling.

Harlequin

An annual subscription to the magazine — 12 issues — costs just $9.00.
Look for the order form on the next page.

Don't miss your copy of North America's most exciting and enchanting magazine!

Subscribe now to the Harlequin Romance readers' own magazine ... Harlequin ... available only through Harlequin Reader Service 12 exciting editions for only $9.00
